"My mother used to tell me stories about a town called Billingsgate. It was built on this island off Wellfleet. Each year, the tides came in higher and higher until finally it was covered by the sea. It's all gone now, but at low tide you can sail out and see the old foundations. And there are still these stories.... Sometimes, on foggy nights, fishermen have seen a light flashing where there's no longer any lighthouse. My mother always said that just because we couldn't see the town, it didn't mean it wasn't still there. When she was growing up here, she was told that if you ever saw the light-house flashing when there was a blue moon, you could go back in time."

I smiled. Since there was no such thing as a blue moon, Molly would never be disappointed. If the idea that a lost village existed under the waves made her happy, what was the harm?

Blue Moon

Blue Moon

HILA FEIL

Harcourt, Inc.

ORLANDO AUSTIN NEW YORK SAN DIEGO TORONTO LONDON

Lyrics from *Singin' In the Rain* used with the kind permission
of Turner Entertainment Co. © 1952 Loew's Inc.
Renewed 1979 by Metro-Goldwyn-Mayer Inc.

First published by Atheneum Books, a division of Simon & Schuster,
New York, in 1990
First Harcourt paperback edition 2007

Library of Congress Cataloging-in-Publication Data
Feil, Hila.
Blue moon/Hila Feil.
p. cm.
Summary: Working on Cape Cod as an au pair, Julia and her young charge,
Molly, sense the mysterious presence of Molly's mother who died years ago.
[1. Supernatural—Fiction.   2. Au pairs—Fiction.   3. Cape Cod (Mass.)—
Fiction.]   I. Title.
PZ7.F3335Bl 2007
[Fic]—dc22   2006050488
ISBN 978-0-15-205933-0

Text set in Minion
Designed by Lauren Rille

H G F E D C B A

Printed in the United States of America

For
NANCY JACKSON

Many thanks to Paula Tasha and Don Brazil
for their help with the sailing sections.

Blue Moon

CHAPTER ONE

June 24th

I am alone now in my room, the summer stretching ahead of me like the empty pages in this notebook. Outside the window there is a thin new moon and I can just make out the humpbacked silhouette of the dunes. There is a scattering of lights, but the darkness hides the ugliness of the new houses. This room, at least, is just what I would have chosen: an iron bedstead, little dormer windows tucked into the sloping ceiling, faded blue flowered wallpaper, and a bathtub with clawed feet. It really is the room for one of those desperate young women in gothic novels who take a job as a governess and find themselves catapulted into romance and adventure.

I know I don't really qualify. I'm not an orphan (although I sometimes feel like one) and my future is not a total blank since it includes (undramatically) my senior year at high school. But this past winter, with my parents' divorce, has certainly brought an end to life as I have known it and made me feel it is dangerous to imagine the future.

When my mother's friend Doris mentioned a summer job as an au pair on Cape Code, I told my mother that I didn't want to spend the summer with people I didn't know and that I don't like little children. I didn't add that I was doubtful about any friends of Doris's. She and my mother were in summer stock together about a hundred years ago. Now Doris appears in commercials as one of those middle-aged women who worry about the spots on their dishes. My mother was once a very young new face in a musical revue, but since the divorce she's been working for a real estate agent. I wasn't particularly looking forward to a summer in New York City while she studies for her broker's exam, but I wasn't too thrilled about her eagerness to ship me out either. Until it occurred to me that it sounded a bit like *Jane Eyre*. I figure that in this day and age, an au pair is as close as you're likely to come to being a governess. Not that I really think anything exciting is going to happen, but I do think that if you're going to be miserable, you might as well be literary about it. And there *is* something strange about this house.

I would have preferred to take the train. In my limited experience, arrivals are likely to be a disappointment, but there's still something dramatic about departures. I could name about a dozen great train scenes from movies or books, but try and think of one memorable departure from the Port Authority Bus Terminal. Unfortunately, the train arrived too late at night, so I had about six hours on a bus whose air conditioning wasn't working to wonder about what was waiting for me at the other end. Given the choice, I would have picked a bleak house on the dunes, the taciturn inmates concealing some dark secret, but since Doris's friend was a soap opera writer with a nine-year-old girl, this didn't seem very likely.

After about five hours, we arrived in Fall River—the place where Lizzie Borden took an ax and gave her parents eighty-one whacks. I was a little disappointed that the bus station was near a perfectly ordinary shopping mall. I know a funny song about Lizzie Borden and how you couldn't chop your mama up in Massachusetts and then blame all the damage on the mice. We used to sing it on car rides in the days when my parents were fun. It's hard to understand how two people who could laugh over a song like that could end up hating each other, but there seems to be a lot I don't understand.

When I finally arrived about an hour later at the bus station in Hyannis, I tried to guess which of the people was there to meet me. None of them seemed very promising. Finally a blond woman wearing sunglasses and a peach jumpsuit came over and asked, "Are you Julia Johnson?" in a doubtful way that made me wonder how my mother had described me. I know I'm not pretty, but I don't think there's anything actually wrong with the way I look. I'm tall, and a bit bony, and since I can't do very much with my hair, I usually yank it back in a long braid. But I do think I have nice eyes (they're an odd kind of gray) if you bother to look behind my wire-rimmed glasses, and I've been told I have good cheekbones, for whatever that's worth. I was wearing clean jeans and a sweatshirt—at least they were clean when I started out. I didn't think I looked like someone you wouldn't trust your child with.

When I admitted to being me, the woman introduced herself as Cheryl Hayes (I thought she looked just like a Cheryl) and introduced the girl at her side as Molly. My first thought was that they didn't match. Cheryl, besides her blondness, had this kind of glossy look that you don't usually see in real life. Everything about her, from her haircut to her clothes, looked expensive and up to the minute—and as if she'd change it as soon as a new look came along. Molly was very dark with almost black hair pulled into two braids. Although she was wearing shorts and a T-shirt with armadillos on it, there was something about her that reminded me of those somber little girls in

Victorian pictures. Maybe it was because she wasn't smiling. She eyed me in a suspicious way, which didn't promise well for the summer, but I thought that if I were she, I wouldn't be crazy about having to spend the summer with someone I didn't know and might hate.

We all climbed into a BMW station wagon and Cheryl set out to make me feel welcome. At least that's what I think she was doing. She told me how glad she was that I had come, and how much she was sure that I was going to love it. The house was right on the bay and there was a tennis court and lots of other neat teenagers and she was sure I would have a great summer. I could tell she is one of those determined people, so there seemed no point in telling her right away that I hate most sports and am likely to despise any teen-agers she thinks are neat. The boys in my school are beneath contempt and my friend Nola is the only one who sees things the way I do.

Cheryl was explaining that the reason she needs someone to look after Molly is that she was promoted to head writer on the soap opera she is writing, when something bit me. I looked down and saw that a small creature covered with spines had sunk its teeth into my hand. Molly quickly removed the animal and put it back in her pocket.

"You have a pet hedgehog?" I asked, wondering what I had gotten myself into.

"I thought I asked you to leave her at home," said Cheryl as she maneuvered the car into a rotary. "I just had the upholstery cleaned."

Molly and I exchanged looks.

"Can I look at her?" I asked. "I've never seen a hedgehog outside of Beatrix Potter."

Molly took the hedgehog out of her pocket. It was now a tight ball of short spines. "Her name is Lucy. She did come from England originally. We found her in this pet shop and couldn't resist."

Actually Cheryl struck me as the kind of person who could easily resist a hedgehog, but perhaps she had a hidden side. Lucy uncurled cautiously and revealed a delicate pointed face with a moist twitching nose and bright black eyes. When I extended a finger toward her she snorted and frowned and the spines on her forehead lowered.

Molly stroked her gently and the spines relaxed and flattened. I thought that Molly and I might hit it off after all.

I had never been to the Cape, but I had this picture of dunes and deserted moors. I guess I'd seen too many photos of J.F.K. at Hyannisport. I wasn't prepared for the rows of motels and gift shops strung along Route 6, the highway that slices down the crooked arm of the Cape. They didn't exactly fit in with my Jane Eyre scenario, but, after all, that was just a game and was bound to come to an end sooner or later.

After almost an hour, we passed a sign for the town of Wellfleet. I imagined we were now somewhere along the wrist of the Cape, nearing Provincetown at the tip. Just after a sign saying we had crossed the Truro town line, Cheryl turned off the highway and down a road with a gold-lettered sign that said SANDPIPER VIEWS. As the road wound through low hills sparsely covered with pine trees, each new house I saw was larger and uglier than the last. Like trees in the jungle, they climbed to absurd heights, in order, I guessed, to catch a glimpse of some view invisible to me. They looked as though they had been designed by a crazed Hollywood art director. Bits and pieces from every period were tacked on—here a carriage lamp, there a widow's walk or a cathedral window—apparently in an effort to suggest the opulence of some other era. I tried to guess which of these belonged to Cheryl. I had picked a throwback to a fifties ranch house that looked as if Barbie and Ken might live there, when we turned into a driveway.

I stared in surprise at the rambling white house that loomed through the trees. While the new houses seemed showy and out of place, this one looked as if it had grown very slowly, with porches and wings added haphazardly over the years. It had obviously seen better days. The white paint and red trim were peeling, and the shingles on the roof were green with moss. Most likely it had once stood alone among the towering elm trees, surveying the scrap of bay now visible through a cleft in the dunes. Like a shabby but still haughty dowager, it seemed to be doing its best to ignore the ugly houses that had invaded its territory. As I dragged my suitcase through the door, I noticed the garden. Bleeding heart, columbine, delphiniums, and lupine mingled with violets in a way that had a kind of haunting loveliness to it. Although it was overgrown now, I thought that whoever had planted it had managed to evoke the melancholy sweetness of a fairy garden in a Victorian engraving. In the middle of the tangle was a sundial. I thought that tomorrow I would like to look at it more closely.

The inside of the house was somehow like the garden. There was very little furniture, and what there was had a sort of beat-up look. None of the chairs matched and the upholstery was either faded or torn. But everywhere there were wonderful things. In the living room was an old rocking horse, a collection of bird decoys, and a weather vane of an old man with a scythe, who seemed a sort of Father Time. Above the brick fireplace in the dining room were a collection of papier mâché skeletons dressed up in funny costumes, and a wooden shadow box, which contained skeleton puppets playing musical instruments.

There was something both playful and strange about the house, which didn't at all match my picture of Cheryl. Although it was unlike any house I had ever been in, I felt an odd recognition, as if I had always wanted my own house to be like this but hadn't known it.

As Cheryl walked me through the rooms, I thought that everything in them seemed chosen with care, for its oddness or charm, and yet the objects didn't intrude on the house itself, whose wide-planked floors and old paneling had a beauty of their own.

Cheryl kept up a kind of tour guide chatter.

"The original house was built in 1810, and the wings and porches were added on later. Our bedrooms are in the old part of the house, and you'll be in the new wing above the laundry room...."

As I looked at a poster at the top of the stairs—a woman in evening dress looking at herself in a mirror and seeing the reflection of a skeleton—it seemed almost as if the house contained a message I couldn't quite read. If it did, whatever it was certainly didn't go with my impression of Cheryl.

I particularly like Molly's room. Like mine, it is nestled in the eaves, with little dormer windows.

It has an old print of Noah's Ark on the wall, and a photograph of Molly when she was younger. She is sitting on a dresser with an antique doll. With her hair loose, she looks like one of those haunted-looking little girls that Lewis Carroll photographed. The picture is actually a reflection in a mirror, so that it looks as if she really has crossed into a looking glass world.

As we started back to the kitchen, I noticed that there was one room with a closed door that we didn't enter. The tour was so complete, including every bathroom, closet, and porch, that I wondered why Cheryl had chosen not to show it to me.

During dinner, Cheryl asked me all those interview questions that I hate about my school and family. When I told her my father is a doctor, it occurred to me that her picture of "doctor" probably has nothing at all to do with the peculiarity of who he really is—how he gave up the allergy practice my mother thought was boring to work for the World Health Organization in Senegal, a place my mother would love to live. Cheryl asked me questions as if she were filing away the answers for some future script, but since she didn't ask the right questions, and I left out all the shadings and complexities, I suspected I would never recognize myself and my family if we ever made it into her series.

I knew I was right when Cheryl suggested we watch a tape of today's show. The soap is called *All Our Days*, and was extremely difficult to follow because there are a great many characters in it who all have the same plastic look, so it's not easy to tell them apart. One man seems to be having trouble making up his mind between a brunette and a blond. They are equally vapid, so it's hard to tell which one you're supposed to like better. Cheryl watched it attentively, as if it were all new to her, but Molly seemed more interested in stroking Lucy, who sniffled around her lap and then curled into a ball. When the man said to the blond, "You've never looked lovelier. I'd like to shower you with flowers," I thought I noticed the trace of a smirk on Molly's face.

Perhaps because of this, later I asked Molly if she would like me to read to her before she went to bed. So far we hadn't exactly made friends and it seemed as if this might be a beginning.

"I can read to myself," she said.

"I'm sure you can," I said, "but I thought maybe it would be fun if we read something together."

"If you want to," she said, as ungraciously as possible. I decided to ignore her tone, and went to her bookshelf. Among the books, I noticed *The Lion, the Witch and the Wardrobe,* which is still one of my favorites.

"What about this?" I asked.

She shrugged, and I decided I might as well please myself. The dust jacket was torn and faded. On the fly leaf, in a child's handwriting, was written, "If this book should chance to roam, box its ears and send it home, to Maria Dyer, Truro, Mass." I wondered if Molly had found it at a yard sale. Lucy crawled under the covers as we read, and a black cat with long hair and wild yellow eyes stalked into the room and sat at the foot of the bed. He glared at me and jumped off when I reached down to pet him. Molly says his name is Tobermory and that he isn't friendly, which I could have figured out for myself. When it was time to turn out the light, Molly put Lucy in a cage beside her bed.

As I tried to find the way to my room through the maze of halls, it occurred to me that I've never spent the night in a house this old. In theory, I've always sort of believed in ghosts. I like the idea of something lingering on, but now I realize that maybe I'm not so ready to put it to the test. Cheryl had gone up to her room, and I didn't actually feel anything untoward as I passed by the empty rooms. And yet, there is something definitely peculiar about this house. Something that doesn't quite add up. As I passed the room that Cheryl didn't show me, I couldn't help turning the knob, but it was locked....

Alone up here, miles from the others, I can't help thinking of mad Bertha Rochester, but obviously that is ridiculous. People like Cheryl don't keep a crazed former wife locked up in a room.... But where is Molly's father? They say he is off somewhere in South America making an industrial film about coffee, but is he really?

This house is noisy, I'll say that much for it. Something is skittering in the walls. Something quite large. And the pipes are making a kind of groaning noise. At least I think it's the pipes. Now the stairs seem to be creaking.... The stairs are definitely creaking. Now the door is pushing open.... I think I finally understand why people have continued to write in their diaries as enemy soldiers came thudding up the stairs. Writing does tend to distance one. Nothing is quite so bad if you think of yourself as a character in someone else's story.... It's only Tobermory. He's cast a disdainful eye at me and stalked out again.

Well, Bertha Rochester or not, I can't help feeling that there is something strange here. I honestly don't expect anything for myself, but at least I can hope for some sort of dark secret after all, so I will have something to fill these pages besides my efforts to avoid tennis.

Chapter Two

June 25th

This morning I woke to the sound of sea gulls. Like certain smells, it brought with it a feeling of anticipation—almost of happiness. For a moment, I was nine again myself, waking by the sea on the first morning of summer vacation. My parents had rented a comfortably funky house on the tip of Long Island. My father and I had looked forward to a summer playing about with the small sailboat that came with the house, but something about the ocean spooked my mother all of a sudden. Because she wouldn't come with us, our excursions in the boat took on a kind of edge. Looking back on it now, I can see that her gaiety that summer had a kind of brittleness to it, and what I had thought of as the last happy summer was really the beginning of the end. So much for anticipation.

Downstairs in the kitchen, Molly and Lucy were eating breakfast. Apparently Cheryl was already upstairs at work. Molly barely looked up as I entered. She was holding a teaspoon in front of Lucy that had something pale and translucent on it.

"What's that?" I asked, as Lucy sucked it up like spaghetti.

"Wax worms," said Molly. "She adores them."

As I made myself tea and toast, Molly alternated between taking spoons of cereal herself and offering wax worms to Lucy, who chewed on them surprisingly loudly. Although Molly used separate spoons, it was still disconcerting. From the sidelong look Molly gave me, I had the impression this was her intention. If she was trying to get on my nerves, she was beginning to succeed.

After Molly had put the container of wax worms back in the fridge, I asked her what she would like to do. She shrugged. "How about going down to the beach?"

"If you want to."

I could see it was going to be a long day, and an even longer summer.

I had already put on a bathing suit under my clothes. While I waited for Molly to change, I wandered out into the garden. It's not as if I have an actual home to be homesick for. I can't begin to imagine where my father is now, and I can imagine only too well my mother trying to memorize a bunch of facts about real estate law. But I certainly didn't feel I belonged here. As I breathed in the scent of the damp earth and the woodsy smell of the flowers, I wondered what the garden had been like when it was first planted. Even though it was growing out of control, you could still see the care that had gone into planting it. Tucked away among the violets and lilies of the valley were some lady's-slippers. I had the feeling that someone had tried to recreate the magical gardens you find in old fairy books. In fact, the present tangle only added to the feeling of wildness, which seemed to me part of the original intention. In the middle was a bronze sundial shaped like a frog on a lily pad. Around its base it said, "I count only happy hours." I wondered how many hours it had counted. There was a feeling of sadness about the house, and about Molly, who except when she was with Lucy, seemed guarded and watchful. And then I realized that, standing in the garden, I felt as though I were not completely alone, but shared something with the person who had planted the garden.

As Molly and I started walking out to the road, I saw that one of the garbage pails had been tipped over, and that rubbish was spread all over the driveway. I thought I caught the ghost of a grin on Molly's face.

"Dogs?" I asked.

"Raccoons."

"Well, we can't leave this mess."

Gingerly, I began picking up wet orange peels while Molly just watched me.

"Aren't you going to help me?"

Sullenly she began picking up crumpled pages of script soaked in coffee grounds. My efforts to win her over certainly hadn't gotten off to a very good start.

At last we began walking down the tarred road, which wound through the low hills to the cleft in the dunes. On the way, we passed a tennis court where a blond girl and a boy of about my own age were swatting a ball back and forth. They glanced up, stared at me blankly, and went back to their game without a smile or a greeting. Once again, I wondered what they found wrong with me. They didn't look like anyone I'd want to be friendly with, but I prefer to do the rejecting myself. On the other hand, it would make things simpler with Cheryl if they were the ones who didn't want to be friends with me.

Molly and I were silent during the walk, which took less than five minutes. I was beginning to feel a bit desperate. Usually I'm the one who is silent and grumpy, and I was beginning to think this whole au pair idea was a big mistake. I'm not cut out for cheering someone else out of a bad mood.

On either side of the cleft in the dunes were two particularly large houses, their enormous decks eclipsing the natural sweep of the dunes. Molly gave them a vicious look as we passed.

"It must have been wonderful before the new houses," I said.

"It was. Then one day they came with a bulldozer and just sliced off the top of the dunes."

Lit by her anger, Molly's face was the most animated I had seen it.

As we came through the cleft in the dunes, the bay was spread out below us. The beach was deserted, and the sand, swept into ripples by the wind, looked clean and untouched. As we climbed down the wooden stairs to the beach, I noticed a small shed with weathered shingles that looked as if it might have belonged to the old house in happier days.

"What's that?" I asked.

"Just an old boathouse. There's nothing in it."

Her tone was sharp and she began walking toward the water. The tide was out, and beyond a sandbar, a single immense rock stuck out of the water, dark and somehow inviting.

"Shall we try to walk out there?" I asked, as we waded out into the water.

"If you don't mind the crabs." She gave me a

sidelong look and I tried not to jump as something skittered across my foot.

"Once there was a nurse shark who was washed in at low tide," said Molly conversationally.

"Really," I said, in the same tone, and fixed my eyes on the bottom, trying to steer clear of the patches of seaweed. From one patch, some murky shapes emerged.

"What are those?" I asked suspiciously.

"Tree trunks. There was once a forest here, but the sea is eating away the land. One day it will all be gone—even the ugly houses."

Small comfort, I thought to myself. There was something eery about the ghostly remains of the forest, but as my eyes became accustomed to the rippling light, I could see that the sandy bottom was filled with busy creatures. Little hermit crabs scuttled along sideways. A larger crab quickly buried itself in the sand as I approached. A school of tiny fish wheeled and darted, obeying some inscrutable impulse. Above us, a tern gave a sharp, insistent cry and dive-bombed a fish, while sea gulls continued to skim below the scattered clouds. Each of these creatures seemed filled with its own importance, believing itself the center of its universe. For a moment, I saw myself as just another part of all this activity, and there was something peaceful about that thought.

We had reached the rock. It was covered with seaweed and barnacles and clinging starfish, already beginning to dry in the sun. Up close, the rock did not have quite the same attraction that it did as a distant goal. Exposed to the air, the creatures from the undersea world had lost some of their mystery. Now it was the shore that seemed remote and interesting. In the other direction, the land curved in a gentle arc. At the very tip, I could barely see the silhouette of some sort of tower.

"What's that?" I asked Molly.

"The Provincetown Monument. It's where the Pilgrims first landed. There was no fresh water, so they went on to Plymouth."

"I was never all that crazy about the Pilgrims," I said. "Maybe I just had a rotten teacher, but they always seemed kind of stuffy and boring. Still, it must have been something to arrive at a completely untouched place."

"It wasn't untouched. There were Indians here. The Pilgrims stole their corn."

"Molly," I said abruptly. "Would you like me to leave?"

"Why?" She seemed surprised.

"From the moment I arrived, I've felt you didn't want me here. It's not all that easy for me either. If you want, I can tell your mother it's not working out, and she can find someone you like better."

"My mother?" Molly looked bewildered.

"Cheryl. I'm sure she can find someone else."

"Cheryl isn't my mother! I wouldn't have a mother like that!"

I didn't point out that we can't choose our mothers because, in fact, that was exactly what had been bothering me. I don't know why I hadn't figured it out before.

"Cheryl's your stepmother!" I said, with an odd feeling of relief.

"Of course. My real mother wasn't anything at all like that. She was a photographer."

As she turned and looked out to sea, I noted the past tense.

"The things in the house," I said, "and the garden, they belonged to your mother. She was the one who bought the hedgehog."

She nodded without turning her head.

"They didn't seem like Cheryl....Neither did you, as a matter of fact."

"Of course not."

"I think I would have liked your mother," I said slowly.

Molly turned and looked at me, almost as if she were seeing me for the first time.

"She wasn't like most other grown-ups....She hated all that." She gestured to the houses that lined the dunes. "We used to try to think up crazy ways to destroy them. But she said in the end it didn't matter. The old Cape is still there if you know how to look."

"How, or where?"

"Both, I guess....She used to tell me stories about a town called Billingsgate. It was built on this island off Wellfleet. Each year, the tides came in higher and higher until finally it was covered by the sea. It's all gone now, but at low tide you can sail out and see the old foundations. And there are still these stories....Sometimes, on foggy nights, fishermen have seen a light flashing where there's no longer any lighthouse. My mother always said that just because we couldn't see the town, it didn't mean it wasn't still there. When she was growing up here, she was told that if you ever saw the lighthouse flashing when there was a blue moon, you could go back in time."

I smiled. Since there was no such thing as a blue moon, Molly would never be disappointed. If the idea that a lost village existed under the waves made her happy, what was the harm?

"Did the house belong to your mother's family?" Perhaps because Cheryl so obviously came from somewhere else, this hadn't occurred to me before.

"Her relatives built it, a long time ago. Their name was Snow. It went out of the family after the First World War. Just before I was born, when the land was going to be subdivided, my father was able to buy it. My parents had been living in Cambridge and they had this idea about living on the Cape...."

Her voice trailed off. I knew all about ideas of

that kind, and I didn't press her. Water was lapping at our toes. The tide was beginning to come in, and I suggested we start back.

The beach was no longer deserted. Two ladies with leathery tans had brought beach chairs and a picnic basket. A frazzled-looking woman surrounded by plastic beach toys was trying to persuade a toddler to build a sand castle, and what was either the kids from the tennis court or their clones were cooking themselves in the sun. The day had a technicolor brightness to it that reminded me of Cheryl's show. Somehow I couldn't imagine anything interesting happening in this glaring light. I wished there were a real-life equivalent to the shadows of an old black-and-white movie.

"Listen, Molly," I said. "You never answered my question. Do you want me to go home?"

She kicked a pebble and watched it clatter down the path.

"No," she murmured.

"I didn't hear you," I said.

She looked up. "I'd like you to stay."

"Good," I said. "I'd like to stay too. Now that's

settled, is there someplace we could go that isn't so…" I trailed off, unable to find a word to describe the people at the beach.

Molly hesitated. "There's the woods," she said, after a beat.

We stopped at the house to change out of our wet suits, then we set out in the opposite direction, away from the bay. Molly soon turned down a narrow sand road that led into the pine woods. I was glad to be out of the sun, but I must admit I was a bit disappointed by the woods. I was used to the Connecticut woods, with their tall hardwood trees and thick underbrush, where as a small child I had sometimes sensed the prickling thrill of unseen presences. These woods, with their scrawny pine trees and scrub oaks, seemed thin and uninhabited by anything except birds and chipmunks. Molly pointed out a clump of Indian pipe, pale and ghostly beneath the trees, and a pink trillium tucked beneath the underbrush. Perhaps with enough time, I would come to appreciate these woods.

Without warning, the road suddenly ended in a clearing. A wrought iron fence, sagging with age, surrounded an old cemetery. The lichen-covered tombstones slanted in every direction. Coming upon it unexpectedly, the graveyard had a dreamlike quality.

"What a strange place for a cemetery," I said.

"I think it once belonged to the house. Some of the original Snows are buried here. It's lovely, isn't it?"

It seemed an odd word for a graveyard, but I realized she was right. A rabbit hopped slowly away from us with no apparent alarm, and a robin trilled once and fluttered to the top of a tomb-stone carved with a finger pointing heavenward. Unlike the vast cemeteries on the way to the New York airports, their raw, new stones suggesting sudden violence, these stones, with their quaint carvings of flowers and angels, did not seem to be so much about death as a reminder that some-thing did survive from the past.

We wandered slowly among the stones, stop-ping to examine the more interesting ones: Little stones with lambs on top of them marked the graves of children, some with peculiar biblical names like Achsah, Huldah and Zaccheus. Others told a story—someone lost at sea, or twins who had died within days of each other. My favorites were two little tombstones with lambs on them that said "Dear Little Bertie," and "My Darling Eugene."

As I walked with Molly to the far end of the graveyard, I wondered why I found it so peaceful. As I studied the gravestones, their carved flowers and mottos only enhanced by the lichen and moss that covered them, it struck me that, as at the old house, the working of time was visible here. But instead of destroying and eroding, it seemed to add a glamorizing patina to the objects it touched.

At the far end of the cemetery, the stones were almost black. They were so worn, it was difficult to make out the inscriptions, but I liked the primitive carvings of angels whose faces looked like skulls. The earliest stone belonged to Jedediah Snow, 1787–1834, and his beloved wife, Rachel. I assumed they must have been the ones to build the house. I tried to empty my mind and concentrate, but I could get no feeling of what they had been like.

I browsed among some of the more recent

Snows. The latest were dated around the Second World War, but they did not have the appeal of the early gravestones. I looked up and realized Molly had wandered to the far side of the graveyard where a grave stood by itself under a large elm tree. I walked toward her and saw that the stone was a plain slab of granite, left rough hewn. All that was written on it was MARIA DYER HAYES.

So the book had belonged to Molly's mother....I found myself wondering about the little girl who had read about another world on the other side of a closet door and had grown up to tell her daughter about a world beneath the sea. What had she been like, and how had she died? The severity of the stone, lacking even dates, suggested that it was concealing something.

Molly looked up as I approached. Her eyes refocused as if she were pulling herself back from a great distance, but her face was unreadable. As we started back, I wondered about Molly's father. What was he like, and what had made him marry two people who seemed as different from each other as Cheryl and the woman beneath this secretive stone?

CHAPTER THREE
June 30th

I am no closer to finding the answers to any of my questions. Instead, I seem to have slipped into a routine in which the days run together and questions of any sort begin to fade.

It's hard to believe I've been here a week. In the early morning, Molly and I go to our beach while we can have it to ourselves. Later, we bike to a small pond in the Wellfleet woods. It's surrounded by trees and has almost no beach and is therefore shunned by the tan-seekers. The only other regulars are an elderly couple and some aging hippies who keep to themselves and don't bother us. I realize I have come to enjoy our guerrilla existence. We have invented a game: We are behind enemy lines, alien observers of the people on holiday. I know I should be beyond this sort of thing, but I seem to have more in common with a slightly weird nine-year-old than with the Ralph Lauren duo at the tennis court.

We have reached a kind of truce with the raccoons. On the second morning, there was garbage spread all over the lawn again.

"Can't you fasten down the lid?" I asked.

"They can open anything," said Molly, with what sounded almost like pride.

"You go through this every morning?"

"It drives Cheryl crazy."

Once again, I thought I caught the ghost of a grin, but I couldn't understand a woman like Cheryl allowing herself to be tyrannized by a bunch of raccoons.

"Well, I'm not going to begin every morning picking up garbage. Isn't there something we can do?"

Molly hesitated. "My mother used to feed them."

"Where?"

"She'd put out a plate near the garbage, with

the things they liked best, and they'd leave the rest alone."

And so every night we raid the fridge for tidbits we think the raccoons will like. We are pleased when they clean their plates, and slightly offended when they don't, but at least they don't tip over the pail anymore. Cheryl hasn't commented—perhaps she hasn't even noticed—but even though the end result is for the best, I have a feeling that in befriending the raccoons, I have taken sides in some battle I don't even understand.

In the evening we watch *All Our Days*. Molly and I never discuss Cheryl, but I think we both realize I am exactly the kind of influence Cheryl wouldn't have chosen if she had taken time to notice who I really am.

I suspect Molly watches the show to collect ammunition against Cheryl. She keeps a running list of her favorite stupid lines. I would never admit this to Molly, but I have actually begun to hope that Lance will choose Sandi, the blond, over Lila, the brunette, who seems a bit clingy. The characters are no less dumb than they were before— they might as well be Barbie and Ken—so there must be something insidious about watching any-thing every day. I shudder to think what I will be like by the end of the summer. It's depressing to think that second-rate fantasy can be as absorbing as the classier stuff. Maybe all we ever do anyway is fill in the blanks.

As a kind of antidote, and to remind myself of who I am (or thought I was), I study Maria's pic-tures. At least I assume they are hers. There are black-and-white prints scattered throughout the house that look as though they were taken by the same person. There is a strangeness, a feeling that the ordinary has become dreamlike, that runs through them all—a caught moment in which a blowing curtain turns a woman into a ghost, a store mannequin who seems more alive than the salesgirl behind her, a bag lady in a crazy hat who stares at the camera with an intensity that makes you think of the hag in a fairy tale who turns out to be the fairy godmother.

Among the clutter on Molly's dresser, there is a snapshot of what I take to be Maria with Molly as a baby. Maria is bending down over Molly, who is sitting in her lap. The wind is blowing her long dark hair around her face, so it's not easy to see her features, but she is smiling. I keep wishing I could make her look up so I could see her better. It's hard to match this smiling young woman with the dark and fantastic vision of her photographs.

I was right about Cheryl's being determined. When she finally realized that Molly and I were not picking up on her hints about the kids at the tennis court, she organized a beach picnic today.

When we got down to the beach, the two kids from the tennis court were already there with their mother, a thin woman with frosted hair who was introduced as Janet. The boy was Todd and the girl was Ashley. Even up close you couldn't see any flaws in them. Their tans set off their perfect features and their blue eyes and blond hair. You could have stuck them right into *All Our Days*. Including their names. I had a moment's satisfaction in thinking that if I were writing the script, I would turn Todd into that blond man in every gothic novel who starts out seeming nice and turns out to be a creep. But of course I've no control over this script, and it's obvious that Sandpiper Views is not the sort of place you're likely to find the more interesting stock character—the dark, scowling stranger who turns out to be the hero despite his first rudeness.

With some lack of subtlety, Cheryl suggested that Todd and I walk down the beach and collect driftwood for the fire. Although it was still light, the color of the sky had begun to deepen and the horizon line was blurred so you couldn't really tell where water ended and sky began. I've always liked twilight. It's an in-between time when it almost seems as if something unexpected might slip through the crack between day and night. As Todd and I trudged down the deserted beach, I wondered what it would be like to walk at sunset with someone who shared my feeling of precariousness, instead of someone who asked me if I preferred tennis or sailing.

By the time we came back, loaded with driftwood, Cheryl and Janet had lit a charcoal fire and had been joined by another woman (the men seemed to come out only on weekends) with a daughter named Laura, who immediately monopolized Todd. They all belonged to the same yacht club and immediately began a conversation about a bunch of kids I didn't know. I sat down next to Molly and tried to ignore the laughter from the other three. I couldn't care less about any of them, or their friends, but as I said before, I do like to do the rejecting myself.

Things improved a bit after it finally got dark. Laura's mother had brought some Portuguese sausage, linguica, which was delicious, and as we all huddled around the fire, I almost felt as if I belonged. The firelight made everyone look more interesting than they did by daylight, and I've always loved the smell of charcoal and burning marshmallows. Then the kids began singing songs I didn't know, and I remembered that I didn't belong here.

I slipped to the outside of the circle. One side of me was still warmed by the fire, but the other side was now brushed by the wind that had blown up off the bay. As I stared at the lights of Provincetown on the horizon, I thought that this seemed

to be my place in things—right on the edge, neither quite in or quite out, and looking into the
distance toward the glimmering lights.

The tide had come in, covering the rock and
the tree trunks, but I knew they were there beneath the silvery ripples, along with Molly's island. Of course, I don't really believe that in some
parallel time children still go to school there,
while the lighthouse keeper tends his light....But
I could see why Molly liked to imagine that there
was something under the surface, a shadow world
unsuspected by these people whose clothes and
conversation belonged in *All Our Days*. I could
feel something in me reaching out to the darkness
below the waves. It was better than listening to the
laughter of the others.

When it was time to leave, we all walked down
to collect water to douse the fire. As I waded into
the bay, I noticed that my feet left a trail of sparks.
Todd said it was some little phosphorescent creatures and suggested we go swimming. The others
immediately pulled off the sweatclothes they had
put on over their bathing suits and plunged in. I

hesitated a moment. Up close, the dark water looked cold and uninviting, but finally I pulled off my own clothes and followed. As I entered the water, I realized that Molly had remained on the shore. I wondered why, but by now I had committed myself.

The water was cold and there was something spooky about its blackness, but as I watched my hands leaving sparkling trails it seemed worth it. My foot touched one of the tree trunks, and I wondered if ghostly birds and squirrels coexisted with the fish. I looked around me and realized that a current was carrying me out past the rock. My above-water head knew that the last thing I wanted to do was to swim any farther out in that black water, but somehow my arms and legs seemed to be following the current, which tugged at me, gentle but insistent, and surprisingly warm.

I knew how things were on the shore. Mostly there was disappointment, and things almost never turned out the way you wanted them to. Was it possible that there was something after all beneath the waves, pulling me toward it? I knew that I should be frightened, but the current was so warm, so gentle. Why not see where it would take me?

"Julia." The voice seemed to come from below the water, kind and welcoming. "Julia!" it repeated. Was I imagining it? I stopped swimming and lifted my head.

"Julia!!" This time there was no doubt about it. It was a real voice, and it sounded really mad. Cheryl must have been calling for some time.

If anything had been there, it was gone, and I turned back toward shore. Now I could feel the current, much stronger than I had realized. I struck out as hard as I could, but didn't feel as if I were moving forward—almost as if the current were resisting me. For the first time, I began to be frightened. What had happened out there, and how was I going to get back? I redoubled my strokes and began to feel I was gaining on the current. Was it my imagination that something had sensed my determination and given up?

By the time I had finally made it back to shore, I decided that was the last time I would go for a night swim.

Cheryl didn't attempt to hide her irritation.

"You can't mess about, Julia. The bay isn't a swimming pool. When the tide turns, there's a much stronger current than you might think."

Molly was silent, and once again, I wondered why she hadn't gone swimming. Usually she was the first one in the water.

Cheryl drove back with the cooking things, but I said I would like to walk, and Molly said she would join me. As we walked up the road, I noticed the first fireflies blinking among the trees. I gave up looking for signs and omens a long time ago, but I was grateful to these tiny dancing creatures for punctuating the night with their fairy lights.

CHAPTER FOUR

July 1st

This morning I woke feeling restless and cranky. It's not that I expected anything different from the beach picnic, but somehow it awakened a picture of what it would be like to share twilight on the beach, or be part of the firelit circle. As I stared at the low gray clouds that had slid over the bay, I wondered about what I had felt while I was swimming. At the time, the feeling that there was something beneath the waves had seemed very real, but today I wasn't sure of anything.

It's not as if I actually believed in Molly's undersea village, but I welcomed anything that suggested there was something after all beneath the bright surface of our technicolor days. I had grumbled about all that boring sun, but now that I finally had an overcast day, there was nothing I wanted to do with it. Since this wasn't a movie and nothing exciting was going to happen, the dark atmospheric clouds simply made things cold and dreary. The one thing I knew was that I didn't want to do any of the things Molly and I usually did.

I'm not sure what made me say to her at breakfast, "I wish we had a boat."

Molly poured some milk in her shredded wheat and gave it a stir.

"We do have a boat," she said, after a long pause.

"You do? How come you never mentioned it?"

She fished out a particularly fat wax worm and offered it to Lucy. "It was mostly my mother's boat. We used to sail together."

"I understand. We'll do something else."

Molly considered, then looked up at me. "No, I'd like to take it out. But do you know how to sail?"

"How big is it?"

"It's just a little Cape Cod catboat, about fourteen feet. It's stored in the old boat house."

"But you said…" I began.

"I know. I didn't know you then.… You don't look like someone who would know how to sail," she added suspiciously.

"You're right. But I read a lot of Arthur Ransome when I was a kid."

"That really gives me confidence."

"And I used to sail with my father. I even took sailing lessons for several summers."

"I guess between the two of us we can handle it. If we don't go too far out."

"How far is Billingsgate?"

She gave me a long look, which I couldn't quite read. "If we have the wind with us, it's an easy sail. We don't even need a chart.…"

"Is there a but?"

She hesitated a moment. "No, let's go."

"I think we ought to tell Cheryl."

Usually we were completely on our own. Cheryl seemed more interested in what was happening in *All Our Days* than what we did with ours. It was understood that once she was in her workroom, she wasn't to be disturbed, but I thought she ought to know that we were going out in a small boat. As I approached her door, I heard her voice and assumed she must be on the phone. I hesitated and heard her say, "I've never stopped loving you...."

I was about to creep away, thinking I'd stumbled on a private conversation, when she said, "You too, Sandi. You've been in my thoughts day and night...."

I suppressed a giggle. She must speak her dialogue out loud while she was writing it. I summoned up my courage and knocked.

"What is it?" She sounded just as annoyed as I thought she would.

"It's me, Julia. I wanted to let you know that Molly and I are going out in the boat."

I opened the door a crack. She was sitting in front of a computer.

"Boat?"

"Molly says there's one stored in the old boat house."

"Maria's boat." It was the first time I had heard her mention Maria's name, and there was something startling about it. "Do you think that's a good idea?"

"I've done a lot of sailing. The wind is light and we'll keep close to shore." If she had meant anything else, I decided to pretend I didn't understand.

Cheryl frowned. Clearly she wasn't happy with the arrangement. On the screen of her computer's monitor, the cursor was blinking in the middle of a sentence. She looked at the insistent cursor, then back at me. Obviously she was anxious to get back to work.

"All right. But stay in close and make sure Molly wears a life preserver."

It was the first time she had shown any motherly concern, but I wondered what else was behind her reluctance.

After putting Lucy in her cage, we started down to the boat house.

The door was covered with spider webs, and I wondered if anyone had been there since Maria's death. I looked at Molly to see how she was taking it, but she was turned away from me, perhaps on purpose.

The boat house was almost empty except for a small wooden sailboat with a wide hull and a shallow draft. It too was covered with spider webs, but on the stern I could make out *Dawn Treader* painted in gold letters.

Some fishing rods and a net leaned against the wall. Hanging from a hook was a black slicker and a sou'wester. Once again I looked at Molly, but she had begun brushing off spider webs.

We each took an end and began dragging the boat down to the beach. It was heavy, and I was glad the water wasn't any father. I had no idea when the boat had last been used and I was worried about leaks, but when we finally got *Dawn Treader* into the water, the seams appeared to be tight.

We began by washing off the rest of the spider webs. Then we stepped the mast and unfurled the sail. There was no jib, and the boom was unusually long, which gave the mainsail an odd but jaunty look.

Molly climbed into the boat and I pushed it out farther and then climbed in myself. As the sail filled with wind and the rudder tugged against the current, I felt my spirits begin to lift. I tried to tune myself to the wind and the tide and found myself thinking about those invisible forces that always seem to be pushing us around. For once, instead of being at their mercy, I felt in control, using them to get where I wanted.

The tide was going out and the rock was already half out of the water. Molly told me that the prevailing wind was from the southwest, but today the wind had swung around to the northeast, which would help us get to Billingsgate at low tide.

"You can be the navigator," I said to Molly.

She had brought a chart from a drawer in the kitchen. The fact of the matter is that I am hopeless about maps, but this looked like a reasonably straightforward trip. We simply had to follow the coast till we passed a kind of promontory called Great Island and a little island called Jeremy Point. Farther out, I could see what looked like a fleet of fishing boats, but there were no other pleasure boats near us. We sailed in silence. I was using all my concentration, getting the feel of a new boat in unfamiliar surroundings, and Molly seemed withdrawn—more the way she had been when I first arrived. I thought she might be thinking about her mother, and for the first time I wondered, like Cheryl, whether indeed this had been such a good idea.

Once I had the hang of the boat, I turned my attention to the water. The surface was lead-colored and opaque. I had no feeling of anything mysterious beneath it, and I couldn't decide whether what I felt was relief or disappointment.

We passed Great Island, which had no houses on it and looked as if it might be an interesting place to explore. After we had passed Jeremy Point, Molly pointed ahead to where gulls were circling.

"That's Billingsgate."

My first reaction was disappointment. It seemed to me that the trip had been much too short and uneventful. I can't tell you what I had been hoping for, but there was nothing like the feeling of the night before. Whatever I had felt pulling me must have been my imagination—a wish for there to be something a little more than my everyday experience.

The water was shallower now. I could see the bottom, and ahead of us was a sandbar. Once again, I was grateful for the shallow draft of *Dawn*

Treader. As we approached, I climbed out of the boat again and dragged it up on the sandbar.

I stared at the waving sea grass and some scattered bricks. Molly had climbed out of the boat too, and stood beside me.

"This is it?" I said.

"You're disappointed." Her tone was neutral.

"I don't know exactly what I was expecting…."

"But you were expecting something more."

"I guess so."

Molly sniffed the air, and her eyes narrowed in concentration.

"What is it?"

"Do you smell something?"

I breathed in.

"A salty smell from the water, a strong smell from the wet sea grass. And…I'm not sure… something sweetish but pungent…"

"A little like furniture polish?"

"Maybe." Did I really smell it, or was it just her suggestion?

"When I first came here," said Molly slowly, "I was like you. I don't know what I expected. I knew Billingsgate was gone. But because of the story, I still expected something more....And then my mother told me this story: In Tibet there's this kind of lost magical kingdom. Lots of people went on expeditions to look for it, but no one ever found it. Or if they stumbled on it by accident, they could never find it again. There was this one Russian expedition—in the middle of these bare mountains, they suddenly smelled the blossoms of fruit trees. The man who was their guide told them it was the fragrance of the magical kingdom—they just weren't able to see it."

A gust of wind blew over the sandbar, and I found myself shivering. Molly continued, "My mother said the thing about this kingdom was that it existed in another dimension. A holy person, who had spent a lifetime of study, would be able to see its temples and gardens, but all we would see were a few rocks."

"You think Billingsgate is like that?"

"Not exactly. I mean it's not holy or anything. But if you could see it in the ordinary way, it wouldn't be magic. And just because you can't see it in the ordinary way doesn't mean it doesn't exist."

"Whatever I smelled, it wasn't what I'd expect from an old New England fishing village. It was more…exotic."

Molly hesitated. "My mother wore this oil from Morocco. It smelled sort of like that."

The smell was gone now. I wondered if I had imagined it. But if I had, how was I able to describe it?

Molly's face was pale. The wind blew her bangs over her eyes, reminding me of the photo of Maria.

"She was here," said Molly quietly. "She's gone now, but I know she was here."

I wasn't sure any longer if I had smelled something or not, but I wondered if I had stirred up something that was better left as it was. I looked at my watch.

"Come on," I said. "It's getting late. We'd better get back before Cheryl starts asking questions."

Chapter Five

When we returned home, there was a truck parked in the driveway. On its side was written HENRY GREENFIELD, ARCHITECT. I was surprised that the look Molly gave it didn't blister its pearl gray paint.

"Who's he?" I asked.

"I hate him. I can't imagine what he's doing here. He's the one who built that hideous house on the hill. The one that looks like the kind of restaurant that serves omelettes with lobster, strawberries, and mint."

I laughed.

"It's not funny," she said. "My mother thought he did more to wreck the Cape than anyone else."

Cheryl was sitting at the kitchen counter with a sandy-haired man with aviator glasses and a mustache. I think that even without Molly's introduction, I would have disliked him on sight. I couldn't help feeling that the glasses and mustache were intended to disguise the fact that he looked like some kind of rodent.

Cheryl introduced me as "our au pair" and he nodded at me without interest. Molly refused to say hello. Instead she pointed to the counter, which was covered with plans.

"What are those?" she said.

"Molly…" Cheryl's tone was warning. Then, in an obvious effort to sound reasonable, "Mr. Greenfield and I are going over some plans. I think it's time for a few changes…."

"Changes!" Molly's voice had risen dangerously.

"We can talk about this later," said Cheryl firmly. "We don't want to waste Mr. Greenfield's time. Julia, why don't you take Molly upstairs…."

Molly's face had lost its color. I wasn't sure what was coming next and I did think it was a good idea to get her out of the kitchen. I took her by the hand and started to walk out the door.

We both stopped dead as we entered the dining room. The walls and the mantel were bare. There was no sign of the papier mâché skeletons or the puppet theater.

"How could she," said Molly, "without telling me first?" and began to cry.

I had never seen her cry before and wasn't sure what to do. "What about a bath?" I said, which is my own remedy when all else fails.

I was surprised at how much I too minded the idea of the house being changed, but I was also worried about what was going to happen next. It was obvious to me that Cheryl was not likely to change her mind once she had decided on something. I thought she was wrong not to have told Molly first. But I was also afraid that challenging her would just make things worse.

"Be careful, Molly," I began as we went downstairs, but I was too late. She banged open the door to the kitchen, where Cheryl was making a pasta sauce with sun-dried tomatoes, and shouted, "Why didn't you tell me? Why did you wait till my father was away?"

Cheryl continued to chop sun-dried tomatoes, her face set. This, I thought, is the real Cheryl.

"Your father and I have had many long conversations, Molly. He agrees with me. Aside from the fact that I see no reason for us all to live in a state of decay, it's not...wholesome for you to remain surrounded by your mother's things. In any event, all we are talking about is a face lift...."

"Face lift!" Molly's voice had risen an octave. "The house doesn't want a face lift."

"Houses don't have opinions, Molly." She dropped the tomatoes into some olive oil.

"This one does."

"That's exactly what I mean." She tried to catch my eye, but I was busy setting the table.

"Why didn't you tell me first?" asked Molly again.

"What would be the point? It's going to happen. It would only have given you extra unhappy days and the illusion that you could change something you can't."

"I want to talk to my father."

"There's no way to reach him now, but he'll be back in a few weeks. You can talk to him all you like, but he agrees with me."

She tossed the pasta in the sauce and set it on the counter.

"I'm not hungry," said Molly and banged out of the room. I started to follow, but Cheryl stopped me.

"Let her be. She needs to work it out."

I wasn't hungry either. I'd never felt more like a rat in my life. I hated what Cheryl was doing and the way she was doing it. I've always prided myself on fighting what I think is injustice. I'm the one who speaks up in class when I think the teacher is being unfair, and I once ended up with a black eye when I tried to stop some bigger boys from teasing a cat. I wasn't afraid of Cheryl, but I was afraid that if I spoke up, she might fire me, and then Molly would be left without a friend. It was the first time I had thought of myself as that, but I realized there was a kind of alliance between us, and I didn't want to abandon her.

"I know it seems harsh," said Cheryl, "but

Molly's attachment to her mother is morbid. It's not really for me to judge, but I don't think Maria was the most positive person, and Molly must accept the fact that she's gone."

I twirled my spaghetti around my fork. Eating Cheryl's food made me feel like a collaborator.

"We waited to start the renovations, because I wanted to give Molly a chance to accept me. But it's not healthy for any of us to continue to live in a house that looks like the inside of a disordered brain."

I was surprised at her imagery and at her tone, which seemed defensive. It didn't seem the moment for me to tell her that I had come to love the house as it was.

"You will try to make Molly understand, won't you?" she continued. "I know I can count on you."

"I'm really very fond of Molly," I said. "I'll do what I can to help her."

I was pleased with this reply, which was the exact truth. Although it was open to interpretation, Cheryl seemed to accept it on her own terms and appeared satisfied.

When I came upstairs with a plate of spaghetti, Molly was lying in bed allowing Lucy to chew the end of her braid. Lucy had a peculiar passion for chewing on hair. Molly thought maybe it reminded her of grass.

"Traitor," said Molly.

"I hate it as much as you do," I said, "but I was afraid that if I said something, Cheryl would decide I was a bad influence and make me leave. Is that what you want?"

"No," she said.

"Me either. Look, Molly. I believe in fighting, but maybe there are some things you can't do anything about. I don't know what I can tell you to make it better. Except that I think it stinks."

For the first time, I kissed her when I said good night.

July 2

I lay awake for a long time, staring at the sloping ceiling of my room and feeling powerless. It seemed to me that the house was restless too. The floors creaked, and the plumbing moaned. A loose shutter banged in the wind. There was a feeling of wakefulness to the house, and I wondered if Cheryl had set something in motion without knowing what she was doing.

This morning, as Molly, Lucy, and I were having breakfast, we were startled by a knock on the door. I went to answer it. On the other side of the door was a man in his late twenties or early thirties. I stared at him stupidly. I am not at my best in the early morning, and we weren't expecting anyone, but it struck me that he wasn't the sort of person you would ever expect—except perhaps in some foreign movie. His slightly irregular features saved him from being obviously handsome, and his hair and his tan were so dark that his eyes, which were a battleship gray, were somehow disturbing.

"Is your mother at home?" he asked.

"My mother!" The insult brought me out of my thoughts, and I wondered if I had been staring.

"Mrs. Hayes," he said patiently, and I thought I must have looked as stupid as I felt.

"Is she expecting you?" I asked, with almost deliberate rudeness.

"I have an appointment," he said, "to talk about the renovations."

"Oh," I said, in what I hoped was an insulting tone.

He followed me into the kitchen, and I went upstairs to get Cheryl. When I came back to tell him that she would be down in a minute, Molly was sullenly eating her cereal, while Lucy snuffled around the man's hand. I noticed the hands. They had long, nicotine-stained fingers, with traces of paint on them. He allowed Lucy to nibble the hair on the back of his hands, but he wasn't smiling. His face had a hard set to it, and I could feel a kind of tension coming from him. It was apparent in his hands, and in a vein pulsing in his neck.

"She'll be down in a moment," I said. "Let's go, Molly. There's no reason for us to stay around."

Molly snatched up Lucy, who seemed reluctant to leave her new friend, and we swept out. I wondered if I caught a glint of amusement in those cold gray eyes.

———

In the driveway was an old Land Rover. The olive green paint was almost the same color as the man's army jacket. He was obviously a sworn enemy, but I had to admit that I liked his taste in cars. The Land Rover was rusty and battered, but its classic boxy shape evoked an image of places I had only dreamed of.

"Who's that?" I asked, with as much contempt as I could muster.

"I've never seen him around here," she said, "but I think he's disgusting."

"That goes without saying," I said.

We stayed away as long as we could, arriving back just in time for dinner. The green Land Rover was gone, but I had assumed it would be.

"When is he going to start?" I asked, thinking it best to know the worst at once.

"He's not," Cheryl said, giving a piece of veal scallopini a vicious slap with a cleaver.

"How come?" I asked, surprised by my mixture of emotions.

"I don't know." She put another piece between two sheets of waxed paper and gave it a whack. "He looked over the plans and the house and said he wasn't the right person for the job." She began to heat some olive oil. "It's just as well, really. All we need is a temperamental carpenter."

As I began to wash the salad, I examined my feelings. I was glad even for this tiny delay. But also, in some way that I didn't understand, I was glad that this man was not going to be the one to wreck the house. On the other hand, it meant I wouldn't see him again. I hated to admit that the thought of this dark man appearing at the house every day had added a touch of interest to the summer.

"You are contemptible," I told myself.

CHAPTER SIX
July 3rd

Today I woke to find cumulous clouds massed
over the bay. The atmosphere pressed down on
us, echoing the mood inside the house. Cheryl
kept saying that she wished it would rain, and
then that she hoped it wouldn't rain tomorrow
and spoil the Fourth of July parade.

Normally, Cheryl is not one of those people
who seem very connected with nature, or even
with what is going on around her. Except for an
afternoon tennis date with Janet, she spends most
of the time in her room working, and I have the
feeling that what's happening in *All Our Days*
makes up most of her reality.

I've noticed that soap operas seem to obey

their own physical laws—from which you may guess I've spent more time watching *All Our Days* than I might care to admit. Some days in the show drag on for a week, while on others, characters travel back and forth from a fictional Central American country during a commercial break. Since there doesn't seem to be a budget for real exteriors, the characters spend most of their time in their brightly lit homes, with occasional excursions to a hospital, a funky restaurant, and a fancy one. The few times they are allowed outdoors, they hover close to some plastic trees. In Middletown (a city that appears to be an hour's drive from either Maine or Montana, depending on the script), there are some generic pine trees, which metamorphose into palms when the characters are whisked to Central America. Presumably because of lighting difficulties, the sun always shines on the characters of *All Our Days*.

All of which is to say that I was surprised Cheryl cared about the weather on the Fourth. I decided it was because, for once, real time and soap opera time coincided. A big *"Days"* scene was to take place at a Fourth of July barbecue, in which Lila tells Lance that she is pregnant. (We had inside information from Cheryl that she wasn't—she was just trying to trap Lance—but later she would turn out to be.)

July 7th

I have never been able to influence the weather in my life, but, needless to say, Cheryl got her wish and nature obliged with a storm that may have exceeded her wishes.

I had just fallen asleep when I was awakened by the first clap of thunder. It was followed by another, which sounded very near, and lightning zigzagged over the dunes. I have always loved thunderstorms, but I didn't know how Molly felt about them.

When I got to her room, she was sitting up in bed, her face pressed against the window. Tobermory was crouched under her bed, and Lucy was curled up in a ball in her lap. When Molly turned toward me, her face was bright with excitement.

"I thought you might be frightened," I said.

"I love storms. So did my mother. We used to try willing them to strike the new houses. I hope this one hits us."

"You don't mean that," I said.

"I do too. I'd rather see this house struck by lightning than have Cheryl get her hands on it."

There was another crash of thunder. The strikes were coming closer now, advancing on the house. One of Molly's hands gripped the windowsill, and I could feel her concentrating—almost as if she were a magnet, drawing the storm to her. Of course that was absurd, but I was beginning to be the kind of afraid where reason goes out the window. There was another crash, and the sound of something splintering. I sat down on the bed. Molly's hand left the windowsill and grabbed mine.

"That was one of the elms," she said. When she turned, I could see the fear in her eyes. "I can't make it stop."

"You're not doing it," I said. "You're a child, and that's a storm. You can't control it."

"My mother said everything is connected."

"I don't care what your mother said." I was beginning to think I could get sick of Maria. "If you think you can control the storm, prove it to me. Make it go away."

"I don't want to."

"Because you know you can't."

"I can too."

"Then show me. Let it go."

She released my hand and stared at the window, streaked with rain. Then she flung herself down on the bed, sending Lucy scurrying under the pillow. Slowly the tension left her. There was another thunderclap, but it didn't seem quite so loud. Molly sat up and looked at me. The next thunderclap was definitely softer. The storm was moving away.

"You see," she said.

We looked at each other and began to giggle nervously.

"I was scared," she whispered.

"So was I," I said.

As I started downstairs, Cheryl's door opened. Her face was blurry with sleep but her hair still looked perfect, and I was amused to see that she was wearing a lacy peignoir like one of the characters in *All Our Days*.

"Is Molly all right?" she asked.

"Fine," I said, wondering if her delay in coming out was due to her brushing her hair and putting on her peignoir.

"Good night, then." Her door closed, and I wondered if she dreamed bright dreams peopled by the characters of *All Our Days,* or whether she pushed the rest of us around into convenient segments broken by commercials.

There was a strange smell in the kitchen, and one of the fluorescent lights I had turned off was now on again. Behind the fridge there was a smudgy zigzag of black. Aside from the smell, everything appeared to be all right, so there seemed no point in disturbing Cheryl....But as I lay awake the smell lingered in my nostrils, as if something had changed in the particles of the air, and I wondered what had actually happened.

This morning was clear and bright, just like a Middletown morning. When Cheryl came downstairs, she was wearing blue pants and a T-shirt with red and white stripes. Her cheerfulness was a bit dampened when she saw the black zigzags behind the fridge and discovered that the stove no longer worked.

When we went outside, we saw that a limb from one of the elms was down. Apparently the lightning had struck the tree, traveled through the ground, and knocked out part of the electrical wiring.

"That settles it," she said. "We'll start in the kitchen."

I looked at Molly, but her face was turned away.

Energized either by the storm, or by the fact that she had decided to take the day off, Cheryl practically pushed us into the BMW and drove into Wellfleet for the parade. Neither Molly nor I was very thrilled by the idea of a parade, or by being on Cheryl's trip, but I think we were both relieved to get away from the house, which was beginning to feel like a combat zone.

When we arrived in Wellfleet, I found myself caught by the holiday spirit in spite of myself. I liked Main Street, with its row of little shops. (Although I wished some of them hadn't been so obviously redone with cute gold-lettered signs, and I wondered why any town needed so many art galleries.) Today the street was lined with people, and flags fluttered from the shops. Little kids perched on their fathers' shoulders, and for once the gap between the summer people and the locals didn't seem quite so obvious. As I was trying to decide how I was so certain which was which, there was a blast of band music.

My idea of a parade was something enormous and commercial, like the Macy's Thanksgiving Day Parade, so I was surprised by this one. The floats were all homemade and had the appeal of a school play. Children from the preschool, dressed as flowers, passed by on an open truck, and the fish market offered an enormous papier mâché lobster and an overweight mermaid.

I had just finished admiring an elaborate sea monster built by members from a co-op art gallery, when I glanced across the street. Among the spectators was the man with the green Land Rover.

Even in the crowd, there was something that set him apart. His eyes were narrowed, which made him look disapproving, but maybe it was just against the brightness of what I had come to think of as Cheryl's sun. Standing next to him was a woman. I couldn't tell much about her face because she was wearing a floppy straw hat and sunglasses, but her long faded skirt and old Indian jewelry had a kind of casual elegance about them—a feeling of genuine style that was lacking in Cheryl's most put-together look. I couldn't decide whether or not they were together, but somehow I suspected they were. Although there was a distance between them, they seemed even farther removed from everyone else.

My thoughts were interrupted by a spray of cold water. A man dressed in a slicker and carrying a squirting papier mâché clam laughed at my expression of surprise. As fire engines wailed down the street, signaling the end of the parade, the crowd began to disperse. I glanced across the street and saw the man with the Land Rover and the woman with the floppy hat walking off together. She reached up and took his elbow in what seemed a proprietary way, but it also seemed to me that he did not lose his air of remoteness.

This evening we drove into Provincetown to see the fireworks. It was the first time I've been there, and it seems like a kind of Greenwich Village by the sea. Along Commercial Street, which runs parallel to the harbor, there are the same little shops selling leather goods and crafts, along with tacky shops selling souvenir mugs and sweatshirts. The parade of people looks the same too—a mixture of arty or eccentric types and the tourists who come to gawk at them. I suspect that some of the larger and better-dressed women were actually men, and I was particularly intrigued by a man with a big bushy beard, dressed in a nurse's uniform, who was ushering people into a show by a female impersonator.

We spent nearly an hour looking at the shops. Cheryl kept wanting to buy Molly things—a pair of earrings, a T-shirt—but Molly always refused. I could see Cheryl beginning to be irritated and trying not to show it, and for once I felt some

sympathy for her. I didn't suppose she had bargained on being left with a sullen nine-year-old
while her husband was off who knows where.
After she gave up on Molly, Cheryl tried to buy
me a pair of Navajo earrings I loved, but felt it
would be disloyal to Molly to accept.

By the time we arrived at a little restaurant
overlooking the bay, none of us was in a very
good mood. The restaurant was dark and decorated with fish nets and pieces of timber from old
ships. Standing around the bar were some men I
thought looked like painters, and two women.
Whether these people were strictly local or not,
they seemed to belong in a way that the summer
people in Wellfleet did not. The women, dressed
in black, with interesting haircuts and jewelry,
had a sophisticated look that I envied. I wondered
what it took to acquire that look of self-possession
and to chat easily with the regulars at the bar.
When Cheryl asked if I'd like a Shirley Temple, I
said I'd prefer a Perrier with lime. By this time,
Cheryl looked as if she would like to dump both
of us in the bay, and I couldn't really blame her. I

wasn't sure I would ever forgive Molly for the loss of those earrings.

The sound of the first fireworks brought us all out on the deck. My grumpiness vanished as I watched the jaded-looking regulars from the bar ooohing and aaahing along with everyone else. As Molly gazed up at the fireworks, which blossomed and scattered into showers of light, her face gradually lost its set look. As always, I was struck by how brief each firework was, and how soon it was all over. But tonight, instead of feeling let down, I thought how fireworks really are a celebration of all the beautiful things that don't last. There was a special word for that, but I couldn't think of it.

As the fireworks unleashed themselves in a final crescendo, the boats in the harbor answered with hooting horns, and the people from the bar applauded along with the rest of us. Then we all began to mill toward our cars, and the magic was over.

As we crawled back in a traffic jam, which tested what was left of Cheryl's good spirits, I remembered the word I had been searching for.

Ephemeral. It was a word I had liked when it turned up on a school vocabulary list, but it isn't the kind of word you use much in ordinary conversation. Nor were my thoughts while watching the fireworks the kind I usually think. It's almost as if I were thinking someone else's thoughts. But, of course, that doesn't make any sense.

CHAPTER SEVEN

July 5th

Before I opened my eyes, I had the feeling of another presence in the room. I opened one eye cautiously. Tobermory was sitting at the foot of my bed, staring at me with his bright yellow eyes. Until now, he had kept out of my way and I only caught glimpses of him at times in the underbrush, or when he slipped into the house for a meal.

"Good morning," I said. As he continued to stare at me with his expressionless eyes, I began to feel uncomfortable and wondered what had brought him up here. His look was so intense that I couldn't help feeling he was trying to communicate something, or was sizing me up for some purpose of his own. I extended a hand, but he immediately jumped down and stalked out of the room.

Molly and Lucy were already eating breakfast. By now the wax worms no longer bothered me. Except when Lucy snorted her displeasure and curled up, it wasn't easy to tell how she felt about things. Chewing wax worms and hair were the two things she obviously enjoyed.

"Tobermory paid me a visit this morning," I said.

"That's strange," said Molly. "He was really my mother's cat. He kind of tolerates me, but he's unfriendly to almost everyone else."

"He wasn't exactly friendly. I almost had the feeling he wanted something. But he has plenty of food."

"Maybe he wants you to stop Cheryl."

I was about to tell her that was crazy, when there was a knock on the kitchen door.

"We're suddenly very popular in the early morning," I said, trying to disguise my agitation. Was it possible that the man with the Land Rover had changed his mind?

"Cheryl's probably found someone else to do her dirty work."

But it was neither. A black woman stood on the threshold, carrying a basket covered with a napkin. Her face was ageless—smooth and un-wrinkled—but her white hair, pulled into a bun, suggested she was not young. There was something almost apparitional about her, as if she belonged to another time and place.

"Mabel!" Molly had pushed past me and flung her arms around her.

"Easy, sugar, you'll squash these muffins." She handed me the basket and returned Molly's hug.

"Mabel used to work here," said Molly. "In the old days."

"Thanks. You make me sound about a hundred years old."

"Before us, I mean. Back in the fifties and early sixties. Afterwards she used to come visit my mother here."

"Cooked for a lot of parties in this kitchen," Mabel said, looking around at the peeling cabinets. "Seemed like the house was always full of people then...." I wondered if she was smelling the remains of ghostly feasts, and if she saw the walls freshly painted, the chrome gleaming.

The door pushed open. Tobermory entered with a chirping meow and began rubbing against Mabel's leg.

"I've never seen him do that," I said.

"Tobermory and I are old friends. Like me and Molly's ma. We have an understanding."

Tobermory meowed again. It seemed half greeting and half conversational.

"What's he saying?" I asked, as if I expected her to understand him.

"He's telling her about the house," said Molly. "What Cheryl's planning to do."

"That so?" said Mabel. I couldn't tell if she was talking to Tobermory or Molly.

"She's going to remodel it," said Molly, "and make it all plastic, like her stupid show."

"Is she now?" I was surprised at Mabel's calm. As if she already knew about it, or it didn't make any difference.

"Don't you care?" I asked. "You've been here longer than anyone."

"Seen a lot of changes." Her face was still smooth and placid. "Doesn't always amount to what you think. Whole Cape is changing, for that matter. Isn't much you can do to stop it."

"It's horrible." Molly looked close to tears.

"I don't know. Can be interesting too. When one thing's ending and another's beginning, it makes a kind of space. Never know exactly what will fill it...."

"But Cheryl's going to ruin the house," I interrupted.

"She's just trying to make her mark. Molly's ma isn't easy to follow. There's a lot to this house—more than she may realize—eh, Tobermory?" She scratched behind his ears, and he closed his eyes in pleasure.

"Well, I have to be off. Just stopped by to see my girl. Thought you might like some of these muffins, made with the first blueberries. Don't fret. It'll take more than your stepmother to get the best of this old house." She gave the bricks behind the stove an affectionate pat, as if she were petting a horse. "Take care now." It wasn't clear whether she was talking to us or to the house. And then she was gone, with Tobermory trotting after her.

"What do you think she meant," I asked, "about change not amounting to what we think?"

"Mabel knows things."

"What sort of things?"

"She's got some Mashpee Indian blood in her. I don't know if that's it, but she knows all about plants and how you can use them for healing and stuff. And it's like she's somehow connected to the house. She always turns up when something is about to happen. She and my mother were real close. She never worked for us but she and my mother were friends. It was like they shared something. Not just the house. She came that morning, before we knew...."

She stopped abruptly. "Let's get out of here. Before Cheryl comes down." She picked up the basket of muffins. "Let's follow the old railway right-of-way today."

"What's that?"

"There used to be a railroad that went all the

way to Provincetown. The tracks are gone now, but you can still follow where they were."

Molly seemed preoccupied as we left the house, and I wondered what old memories Mabel had stirred up. But once we were beneath the trees, she seemed brighter. Even I was beginning to like the woods. Though they still lacked mystery, the trees screened us from the vacationers, and I felt closer to the way things had once been.

"My mother and I used to explore here," Molly said after a bit. "We once found this great dump, filled with antique bottles and stuff. There was even this rusty old train set. It was kind of like finding a pirate's hoard."

We walked in silence for a bit, and I wondered if she were remembering walking with Maria, who seemed to have been able to bring excitement to the simplest things.

Suddenly Molly pointed. "You see that?"

All I could see was a patch of bright yellow flowers.

"They look like the flowers near the tennis court. They're all over."

"They're coreopsis. But coreopsis doesn't grow in the woods."

"Oh. I'm not much on wild flowers."

"My mother told me this really weird story. Want to hear it?"

It was obvious she was going to tell me anyway, so I said, "Sure."

"When my mother was a little girl, her family lived in this old house in Truro. At night she used to hear someone walking on the stairs, but there was never anyone there. Finally she learned that there was this old lady who had lived in the house who was hit by a train."

"Yuck," I said.

"No, listen. The place where she was hit was bare. Nothing would grow there. Then one spring the noises stopped. My mother didn't hear anyone on the stairs anymore. She almost missed it. But when she visited the scene of the accident— right here—it was covered with coreopsis!"

I looked at her skeptically.

"You don't believe me?"

I didn't know whether I believed her or not but suddenly I felt closed in by the woods and I had had enough of ghostly meals, ghostly trains, and ghostly old ladies. I wanted to see the sun again.

I got my wish sooner than I expected. Molly stopped abruptly. "Those beasts!"

We had come to a cleared patch. The pines on either side had been hacked down, and in the middle of the clearing was the skeleton of a house. It was only partially framed, but it was obvious that it was going to be gigantic and grotesque. On one side there was a partially shingled tower that looked like a cross between a silo and something Rapunzel might lean out of. The site had appeared to be deserted, but suddenly there was the sound of hammering.

I looked up. Half hidden by the shingles already in place, a man was hammering. The sun was behind him, but there was something familiar about the silhouette of roughly curling hair. Masked by the trees was a glimpse of something that could have been an olive green Land Rover.

"Who designs these things?" I said, in a voice that was meant to carry. "It looks like a reject from Disneyland!"

"It must have been designed by Dopey!" said Molly, even more loudly. I couldn't tell whether she had recognized him too, or was just following my cue.

"Let's go," I said, "before our day is completely ruined."

As we turned back toward the railroad right-of-way, I thought I could feel eyes following us, but I wasn't sure. Suddenly I felt embarrassed. The house was undeniably hideous, but my comments seemed childish and stupid, and I wished I had at least been clever.

When we got back to the house, there was a van parked in the driveway that said C & D CONSTRUCTION. We opened the kitchen door and stared. The butcher-block counter in the middle of the room was gone, and the cabinet next to the sink had been removed, leaving a scarred wall. A red-faced man on a ladder was scraping peeling paint from the ceiling, while another was attacking the second cabinet. As he ripped out the nails, they made a kind of moaning sound.

"No!" I said, involuntarily.

The man on the ladder turned to look at us.

"Hiya, girls! Looks like you'll be cooking out for a while."

But Molly had run out of the house. I turned and ran after her, without saying anything to the men.

CHAPTER EIGHT

July 6th

This morning, as if by unspoken agreement, Molly and I woke earlier than usual. We wanted to be gone before the workmen arrived.

"Where to?" I asked. The beach seemed too close to the house, and I didn't want to walk on the old railroad cut. It might look as if I were hoping to see the man with the Land Rover again.

"What about taking *Dawn Treader* and going for a picnic on Great Island?"

"Good idea." I had been intrigued by the deserted-looking island when we had sailed to Billingsgate.

As we walked down to the beach, we passed Todd and Ashley carrying tennis racquets.

"I see you're beginning to do some remodeling," said Ashley. "The old place will look really neat when it's fixed up."

"Jerk," said Molly after we had passed.

Even though we had taken *Dawn Treader* out a few times, I still thought of her as Maria's boat. I had never asked who had named her, but I had always assumed it was Maria herself. Molly and I were still reading *The Lion, the Witch and the Wardrobe,* and I didn't remember much about *The Voyage of the Dawn Treader* except that it was about the ship that carried Reepicheep, the swashbuckling mouse, out of Narnia and into Aslan, the lion's, country, and that I had cried at the end. Today I thought that Dawn Treader was a name that someone would pick who had not quite grown up. Someone who might not have Mabel's philosophic point of view about what was being done to her house. It occurred to me that if I could get Mabel on her own, I might find answers to some of the questions about Maria that had been puzzling me.

Out on the open water, I began to feel better again. The wind seemed to clear my head, and the flap of the sail and the pull of the tiller restored my sense of well-being.

"Why hasn't Great Island been built up?" I asked, as it came into view.

"It's National Seashore now. Part of the Cape is owned by the National Park Service, and nothing more can be built there. It used to be owned by an eccentric old lady who willed it to the Seashore when she died. My mother said she used to mine the beach so no one could land there."

"Is that true?"

"It used to get pretty weird here, if you believe all the stories. I think it's the long dark winters. Look at that Provincetown man who chopped up a bunch of young girls and buried them in the woods. Right near our cemetery, as a matter of fact."

"No!"

"Oh yes. That I know is true. I can't remember his name but everyone who knew him said he was very nice. I think he was a painter. I don't know about the lady with the land mines. Maybe she just said it was mined to scare people off."

We sailed in silence for a while. I hadn't really thought about this other Cape Cod.

"What's it like here in the winter?"

"Most of *them* leave. And it gets dark around three-thirty."

"It sounds a bit grim."

"I guess it can be. A lot of people take to drink. My mother always said it was the best time. She thought the Cape was most like itself when it was overcast or foggy."

"What about your father?"

"He travels a lot for his work....Oh, good. There's no one else."

We had almost reached Great Island, and I guessed that Molly was letting me know that I had asked enough personal questions. We dragged the boat up onto the pebbly beach and began to explore. I liked the feeling that we had the island to ourselves, but there was something barren about the place, which gave me the feeling that there was nothing to discover. Despite the story about the old lady with the land mines, I had the feeling that nothing much had ever happened here, and nothing much ever would.

We followed a path through the low dunes and ate our lunch on the other side of the island, watching sandpipers and plovers skittering along the shore. Somewhere out beyond us was Billingsgate, but I had no desire to return there. I realized I liked it much better as an idea than as a tumble of old bricks. Is there nothing that lives up to what I can imagine?

As we ate our sandwiches, I thought about this other, wintertime, Cape. As unconcerned as Cheryl seemed about what went on around her, I somehow didn't see her spending the winter in this desolate place.

"How does Cheryl like it in the winter?" I asked.

"Last winter was her first. And she says it will be her last."

Molly's face warned me I was on dangerous ground, but finally some of the pieces were beginning to fit together. Cheryl must have only been married to Molly's father about a year, but how long ago had Maria died? Despite the warning, I couldn't resist asking the obvious question.

"But where will you go then?"

"Cheryl wants me to go to boarding school.

So she can either be in New York or travel with my father."

Molly's face and voice were neutral, but I thought I saw a film of tears in her eyes.

"Boarding school could be fun," I tried. "There are some neat ones where you look after farm animals and stuff...."

Molly just gave me a look and crammed the garbage back into the plastic bag.

"Let's explore the rest of the island."

We covered the other side of the island, but by now a heaviness had settled over us. Although unspoken, it had been clear from the beginning that we were here because we wanted to escape the house. Now the question of next winter hung in the air as well.

At last we had explored everything there was to explore. We had swum, and sat on the beach, and finally there was nothing for it but to return.

We were silent on the trip back. I was sorry I had mentioned next winter. Things were hard enough for Molly in the present.

There were still a few people on the beach, trying to catch the last rays of sun.

"Had a nice sail?" asked one of the blue-haired ladies. But neither of us felt obliged to answer.

When we got back to the house, the van was still there. I looked at Molly.

"We have to face it sooner or later."

As we pushed open the door, we heard the sound of raised voices.

"I'm not interested in excuses," said Cheryl's voice. "You'll simply have to scrape it and do it over again."

"It went on perfectly smoothly. I've never seen anything like it." The red-faced man was standing in the middle of the room, looking at the ceiling. The fresh paint—a salmon pink that Cheryl claimed was an authentic Colonial color, although I had my doubts—had blistered, leaving little bubbles.

"Obviously it was incompatible paint," said Cheryl. "Or the plaster wasn't dry."

"They're both latex," said the man stubbornly. "Of course I checked. And the plaster was dry."

"I don't have time for this," said Cheryl. "I have a deadline. Just fix it."

As she stomped out of the room, the two

men exchanged looks. One of them raised an eyebrow with a clear, "Who does she think she is?" expression.

"It doesn't make sense," said the red-faced man.

"There's a lot about his house doesn't make sense," said the other man. "You ever talk to the guys who put in the new pipes after that freeze-up about ten years ago? Wasn't anyone who went down into the crawl space under the house who wanted to go back again. Nothing particular. Just weren't in no hurry to go back....No offense, Miss," he turned to Molly, "just something about this house."

"It doesn't want to be painted," she said.

He smiled. "There's a reason, I'm sure. But I admit I don't understand it....Well, we'll deal with it in the morning. 'Night girls."

As the door closed behind them, Molly looked at me in triumph. "I knew she'd never let it happen."

"Who?"

"My mother. I knew she'd find a way to stop them."

CHAPTER NINE

July 16th

I will blame the weather. Really, I can't think of anything else to explain the strangeness of the past ten days, or why I haven't felt like writing.

Obviously I don't believe for one moment that Maria is working from the other side to stop the house from being remodeled. And yet it does seem as if something is trying to prevent it.

Of course this is a silly, fanciful way of putting it. What it must be is something to do with this sudden turn in the weather. Some kind of warm front has moved in and refused to move out. Wherever people meet—on the beach, or on Main Street—all they can moan is, "it isn't the heat, it's the humidity," as if this were an original remark. The dampness has brought out swarms of mosquitoes and little no-see-ums, which come through the screens at night. Mildew grows everywhere, even inside my shoes, so I ask you, is it any wonder that paint continues to peel, plaster to crack, and the new tiles in the kitchen to pop up even as you look at them?

I would like to believe that I am the only rational person in this house, but sleepless nights, tormented by small biting things, have taken their toll on me as well. Cheryl's cheerful veneer has cracked, and she is in a perpetual temper. She finally fired the first contractors, but the second ones are having the same problems. I can feel all her determination pitted against the house, and the house pitted against her. No. I refuse to sound like Molly....

I suppose that, little by little, Cheryl is winning. Inroads are being made, but she has also had to give up something. In each room there remains a flaw—a crack, a place that is peeling— like a little signature of some sort.... I know that it is simply because of the damp, but Molly says it reminds her of something Maria told her about the Navajos, who always wove an imperfection into their carpets because they believed that only the gods could create something perfect.

The more frazzled Cheryl becomes, the more triumphant Molly seems. Is that the right word? Yes, I think it is. She has a kind of glow about her now, which sometimes frightens me. I know she believes that all the problems are somehow Maria's doing. If I were a responsible person, a grown-up, I would do something about this. I would talk to her about facing reality or something. But I am not a grown-up, and I am not sure what is the right thing to do. If it makes her happy to believe that her mother has come back in some way, is there anything wrong in that?

The fact of the matter is that now I have something else to think about. Something so unexpected that it drives out everything else.

Tonight Molly said she wanted to read to herself. Although we still spend our days together, I can feel her pulling away from me. Perhaps, reading the book Maria owned as a child makes Molly feel closer to her. Probably I should interfere with this. It's just the kind of thing Cheryl would consider "unwholesome." But the heavy atmosphere in the house was getting on my nerves, and I decided to go for a walk on the beach.

Last light still lingered. Or not so much light, as a luminous glow in the sky. The beach was deserted and there was a breath of wind off the water. I settled myself in a large pit dug by some industrious children and gazed at the lights of Provincetown, and a searchlight from one of the lighthouses, which swept the sky at regular intervals. I wouldn't say that I was exactly happy, but I did feel a kind of contentment. It was a relief to be out of the house, not worrying about Molly. As I became quiet inside, it seemed to me that I could almost feel the tug of the moon on the tide. The pull was gentle and natural, unlike whatever was at work in the house. I was beginning to drift with it, when I was aware of movement on the beach.

It was dark now, but I could make out the darker silhouette of a man and the glow of his cigarette. I was annoyed at the intrusion, doubt-less some late-returning fisherman, and lay low in my hollow.

Footsteps scrunched near to me. I looked up and found myself about to be stepped on by the Land Rover man.

I sat up suddenly, and he looked startled himself.

"I'm terribly sorry," he said. "I thought you were some flotsam."

"Thanks," I said.

"Nothing personal. You were in shadow, and I usually have the beach to myself at this hour."

"I beg your pardon," I said huffily. "I didn't re-alize it was your private place."

"You *are* touchy, aren't you?" I couldn't tell if he was laughing at me in the dark. "I won't offer you a cigarette because it's a filthy habit, but may I sit down?"

I couldn't think of anything intelligent to say, so I just gestured. He sat down next to me on the sand and took another drag on his cigarette. I watched the tip glow brighter, and the smell of the smoke mingled with the salt air. He puffed for a little while in silence, and I wondered why he had chosen to join me. It occurred to me that if I knew him, the silence could have been intimate and companionable, but I was aware of his complete unknownness.

"I don't understand," I began.

"Really?" he said. "Something in particular, or things in general?"

"Why you turned down the job on the house."

"You mean a tasteless person like me who will work on houses designed in Disneyland?"

I blushed, but I suppose he couldn't see it in the dark. "I didn't really mean…"

"Of course you did. And you were perfectly right. The house is an abomination. And that's a very good description, by the way. But that house is what it is, and never was, or will be, anything different. Those of us who live on the Cape year-round try to profit from the summer people where we can. But the old Snow house is something else. As much as I could use the money, I guess we all have a line we refuse to cross."

"So you see it that way too."

"You mustn't be quite so hasty in your judgments, young lady."

"My name is Julia," I said.

"Mine is Sean. Are you a friend of the family?"

"They're friends of friends. I'm a sort of au pair."

"Cheryl doesn't strike me as a person who would tolerate a 'sort of' of any description."

"Well, I do look after Molly. At least I think I keep her company. I just don't feel like an au pair."

"What does an au pair feel like?"

"Someone blond and European and rather flighty."

"Who runs off with the husband. You, on the other hand, are dark and serious. Jane Eyre, or the narrator of *Rebecca*. I think Mr. Rochester or Max de Winter are more your style."

"You're making fun of me again."

"I beg your pardon. I didn't mean to. It's just that I haven't spoken to someone as...untouched as you for a long time."

"Thanks a lot."

"I suppose it's no good my trying to explain

that was meant as a compliment—even six-year-olds seem jaded these days. But since I can't seem to say anything without insulting you, perhaps I'd better keep quiet." He stubbed out his cigarette in the sand, and I became aware of another smell.

"You're a painter," I said.

"What makes you think so?"

"Your jacket smells of turpentine. And there's a sketch pad in your pocket."

"Elementary. When I'm not building ugly houses, that is."

"But surely you don't paint at night."

"Just before. Last light is my specialty."

"That doesn't make for a very long working day."

"That's why I make a point of catching it every day.... Isn't it past your bedtime or something?"

I didn't understand why he seemed anxious to get rid of me all of a sudden, and was going to say I wasn't a child, but decided he'd only accuse me of being touchy again, so I stood up.

"I'll walk you to the stairs," he said.

"Which way do you go?" I asked.

"Down the beach a bit. But I like that rock out

in the water. There was a photographer who took pictures of the same tree over and over. I'm making a career out of the rock."

"I'd like to see what you make of it sometime."

"Sometime. Good night."

We'd reached the stairs that led up the cleft in the dunes. At the top of them, I turned and saw the glow of his cigarette moving down the beach.

I wish I hadn't said I'd like to see his work. It sounds like I wanted to see him again or something.

Chapter Ten

July 17th

This morning I woke with the feeling that something had changed. As I tried to shake off sleep, I thought perhaps the weather had broken, but it was still as hot and heavy as before. As I threw off my clammy sheets, I remembered the conversation last night. A conversation, that was all. Nothing had changed.

Molly was outside on the deck eating a banana. Since the transformation of the kitchen, she and I spend as little time as possible in it. I suppose the contractors did a good job, considering what they were working against. The kitchen would look great in a magazine. The contractors have replaced the old cabinets with some new cabinets stained to look old. Cheryl had them stencil a pattern of pineapples on the walls, and put up a cow weather vane and a lot of shiny copper pots and molds, which she never uses. The thing she is proudest of is an old stove, which she restored at great expense so that it now looks like a reproduction. All these things seem to be trying so hard to look old-fashioned and cozy that it reminds me of one of those restaurants that spring up overnight and try to pretend they've been there for years. I found myself missing the peeling paint and blackened pots of the old kitchen, which seemed to me like the heart of the house.

I was glad when Molly chose to bike to the pond in the woods instead of our own beach. I didn't want to be reminded of my conversation with Sean, which was likely to be our last, because I certainly wasn't going to go down there again this evening.

Wellfleet was already crowded with people, who all had the same idea of shopping before the heat and the crowds. There was an edgy quality about them, as if whatever they had expected of their vacation wasn't happening. For once, I felt we had something in common.

My own edginess dissipated a bit when we reached the pond, and we spent a pleasant afternoon swimming and trying to catch frogs. I was always afraid of hurting them so most of them slipped through my fingers, but Molly turned out to be an expert frog catcher. As she stalked along the edge of the pond, she looked like an oversized wading bird. Her glee when she successfully pounced on one was as happy as I'd seen her. Up close, we admired the flecks of gilt in the frog's eye and the details in the mottling of the shiny green skin, like the finest enamel work. Molly always released the frog at once. It was only the difficulty of catching the slippery creatures that interested her.

When we got back to the house in the late afternoon, the car was gone and Cheryl had left a note saying that she was at a cocktail party and wouldn't be back until after dinner. Molly and I were both tired from all the biking we had done, and after we had eaten the cold supper Cheryl had left out, Molly said she wanted to go up to her room and read.

I went up to my room and tried to read myself, but after I had reread the same paragraph three times without taking in a single word, I had to admit I wasn't concentrating. I still felt restless, but I was afraid that if I walked down to the beach, it would look as if I were hoping to run into Sean. I picked up the book again, but it was no use.

"Well, I'm not going to not go down to the beach just because I think he might be there. That's making too much of it."

I told Molly I was going for a short walk to get some air.

As I started down to the beach, the sky seemed to contain both the light of the day and the promise of night. The cirrus clouds that streaked the sky were tinged with pink and the dune grass was tipped with gold. It seemed to me that I was seeing the colors, and the translucent quality of the light, with a new acuteness. I felt the clumsiness of my words, which could not express my feeling that day and night were balanced on a cusp that was somehow charged with possibility. I wished I were able to paint, and could capture something of the magic this light contained for me.

The beach was empty, except for a man in an army jacket, his back toward me. "I will turn back now," I thought, "or walk in the opposite direction." But somehow these thoughts did not communicate with my feet, which seemed to be walking down the stairs and toward the man.

"Good evening," he said without looking around.

"How did you know it was me?" I asked.

"You were the most likely candidate for a solitary walk. And you move in a cloud of tentativeness. I can hear it in your footsteps."

"I didn't want to disturb you," I said.

"Then you wouldn't have come in this direction, would you?"

I started to turn back.

"Don't get huffy again. I'm glad you did. I just want to make the most of this light."

"But it's black and white!" I blurted out. I could see his sketch pad now. He was working in charcoal, and all I could make out were black and white smudges.

"You were hoping for all those pretty pinks?"

"Not exactly...."

"Do me a favor. Just sit quietly for fifteen minutes, like a good child, and then we'll talk."

"Child" was even worse than "young lady," but my stupid feet, which had brought me down here, had now planted themselves in the sand and I was sitting. I watched the colors in the sky intensifying and then ebbing, and I watched the black smudges on the paper with deepening disappointment.

"You hate it," he said at last as he closed his sketchbook.

"I don't really know much about painting...."

"But you know what you like."

"I'm not as stupid as you think I am," I began.

"What do you think I am? Dumb or something?" he said, in a good imitation of Lena Lamont.

"You like *Singin' in the Rain*?" I asked, surprised.

"Why not? It's the best, except for Fred Astaire."

My astonishment must have showed.

"Oh, you thought I only liked dark foreign movies?"

"You're making fun of me again," I said.

"I'm sorry. I seem doomed to offend you, and disappoint you. You're the last idealist."

"I'm not any of those things," I said. "It's just that as I was walking down here, I was noticing the colors and the light. And thinking how…precarious it was.…I wished I were able to catch that feeling."

"What makes you think I'm not trying to do the same thing?"

"It was colors I was seeing."

"It was light and shadow. I've worked in almost every medium you can think of—oils, water colors, pastels, tempera, acrylics. I've done some very pretty pictures. But they weren't going anywhere. They were just paler reflections of the original, which didn't approach the mystery."

"What mystery?"

"The one you were trying to find words for. When I was younger, I got hooked on painting interstices."

"What's that?"

"The spaces between things. It's another way of seeing. If you paint the space around objects, the objects themselves are revealed in a different way. You can do the same thing with shadow. It's another way of understanding light."

"I think I see," I said, frowning with my effort to follow him.

"Don't look so worried," he said, smoothing out my frown with his finger. I was recovering from my surprise at being touched when he suddenly leaned over and snatched off my glasses.

"I thought so," he said, while I blinked stupidly at him. "One day you're going to be quite something."

"You make me sound like an unfinished piece of work."

"You are. It's all there, but you haven't discovered it yet. I'd love to try to catch that...." He looked at me appraisingly for a moment and took a puff of his cigarette. "Yes," he said thoughtfully. "It's been a long time since I've worked from a figure, but I believe I'd like to try. Would you sit for me?"

I was so astonished that I retreated into my

usual flipness. "Do you want to paint the space around me, or the shadows?" I asked.

"Both."

"I thought you specialized in rocks."

"It's all the same. Behind what look like smudges to you are years of drawing. I'd like to experiment with that again."

"I don't know that I feel like being an experiment."

"Is your time that precious? What are your hours with Cheryl?"

"I'm just supposed to spend the mornings and afternoons with Molly."

"And your free time is all booked, I suppose."

"Okay. I'll try it. Once anyway. But I warn you, I'm a very fidgety sort of person."

"I think I can handle that. Come tomorrow, around seven. There'll still be light."

"I'll have to ask Cheryl, but I think it will be okay."

"Good. I'll see you then."

"But I don't know where you live."

"That's true, you don't. Just keep walking right along the beach to the next set of stairs.

There's an old Cape up in the dunes with a sign that says Holloway. I live in the studio in the back."

"And if I can't come?"

"You can phone me. I'm in the book under Perreira."

"Sean Perreira?"

"I'm what's left of a summer romance," he said. "My mother was a vacationing fine arts major. My father is a Portuguese fisherman. See you tomorrow."

"I'll try," I said. But he was already walking down the beach.

Chapter Eleven

July 18th

I'm not sure why I lied to Cheryl about where I was going. I hadn't even known I was going to, until she came down to the kitchen to get a second cup of coffee. If Molly had been there, I probably wouldn't have done it, but she was upstairs cleaning Lucy's cage.

"I'd like to go off today around seven," I found myself saying. "I met some girls on the beach who invited me to a barbecue."

"Oh, who?"

"They're only here for a week," my voice said glibly. "They're not really in Sandpiper Views. They're in the square white house up in the dunes."

"That's nice," said Cheryl. "I'm glad to see you're beginning to mix with kids your own age. Perhaps you'd like to ask Ashley and Todd over some afternoon."

"Mmmmm," I said, running out before she could press that point or ask any more questions.

For the rest of the day, as I swam again with Molly in the pond and tried to pretend I was interested in catching frogs, I wondered why I had chosen to conceal the truth. Did I think Cheryl would disapprove of Sean because he had refused to work on the house? When I decided not to tell Molly either, I knew that part of the reason was that I wanted to keep it to myself. Sean interested me in a way I found unsettling, and I didn't want to be under scrutiny.

After dinner, I told Molly that I was going for a long walk. Once, I think she might have asked questions, but ever since the renovations began, she has seemed withdrawn and, except when she is catching frogs, uninterested in what goes on around her. I know that I ought to find out what is bothering her (which is obvious) and try to cheer her up (which seems almost impossible), but at the moment her lack of interest is convenient for me. I was glad when she said she was going up to her room. I didn't want her to question the change I intended to make in my appearance.

As I soaked in my bathtub with the clawed feet, I thought what a versatile prop it is, appropriate either to a poor governess or an artist's model in some Parisian garret. After I shampooed my hair, I let it hang loose instead of pulling it back into a braid. As I started to get dressed, I had a horrifying thought. Surely he hadn't meant that he wanted to draw me without my clothes? I couldn't really imagine anyone wanting to draw my bony body. Nevertheless, I found myself putting on my best underwear. If worst came to worst, I would brazen it out and pretend I had a long history of posting as a nude model.

The next question was what to wear. After having pulled on and off half my wardrobe, I settled on a T-shirt with a deep V neck, and my favorite jeans. No one could accuse me of being overdressed, but I knew I looked good in it, and the deep muted blue of the shirt reminded me of twilight. After deliberation, I put on a bit of smoky eyeshadow and some mascara. Without my glasses, the face that looked back at me was slightly out of focus. I wondered if the blurred shadows were the way Sean looked at the world, and if that was how he would paint me. The softened image, with eyes enlarged by the shadow, and my loose hair lent me a kind prettiness that seemed to belong to someone else. I found myself missing my familiar hard edges, and crossed my eyes and waggled my tongue at the image in the mirror as I turned away from it.

Todd and Ashley were playing tennis with their parents. They looked up as I passed, and I waved to them, buoyed up by the feeling that I was on my way to a secret assignation, and thinking that "artist's model" had a pleasantly worldly sound to it.

Molly and I had never explored the other staircases that led up into the dunes. We had no interest in other houses. At the top of the stairs was a boxy white house that would probably have been considered "modern" in the fifties—the house in which I was supposed to be having my fictitious barbecue. I gave it a nod and continued along the sandy road until I came to an old Cape that had HOLLOWAY painted on an oar in front of it.

An elderly woman in a canvas hat was picking dead heads off the roses in a fierce way. Her blue eyes looked at me sharply.

"I'm looking for Sean," I said, timid under her gaze.

"Around the back," she said, "in the studio."

As I walked down the path, I could feel her watching me. Behind the house was a small building that might once have been a barn. Its weathered shingles looked as if they had been silvered by years of wind off the water, and I couldn't help thinking of the description of Wuthering Heights. The rolling dunes, covered with cranberries, had a kind of moorish look to them. This, I thought, was what I had imagined when I was traveling to the Cape.

I knocked on the blue-gray door, and a voice called, "Come in!"

Sean was at the sink, cleaning some brushes, his back toward me, which gave me a chance to look around. The studio was almost empty. Outside the kitchen alcove, the only furniture in it was a futon bed in the corner, an old pine table with four straight-backed chairs, and a potbellied stove. Beneath the windows were some bookcases that looked as if they had been made out of wood found on the beach. The room had the coziness and neatness of a ship's cabin. The colors were all the colors of the dunes, except for a pitcher of bright yellow coreopsis on the table. On one wall was an angry-looking painting. All the shapes were jagged and the dark grays sullen. I might have thought it was an abstraction, if a black triangle in the center hadn't reminded me of the rock. Tacked to the walls were some more of the black and white sunsets. I was beginning to think I had made a big mistake in coming when Sean turned around.

"You hate it, right?"

"It looks...violent."

He looked at the painting. "Not one of my better days. And not one of my most successful paintings. I keep it up as a reminder."

"Of a bad day?"

"Of how far I have to go. There's a lot to be

learned from failures....Now let's see what we'll do with you."

His tone was businesslike. He looked at me appraisingly, eyes narrowed.

"I think we'll put you in one of the chairs," he said. "Here, where we can get the light through the window." So much for my fears about having to take off my clothes. "Turn your head a bit to the right. Now back. Good."

He picked up a piece of charcoal and began to draw. It was a curious sensation, to be the object of such intense but impersonal scrutiny, like that of a baby or an animal. I wondered if he was drawing the space around me, or building an image out of shadows. Was I nothing but a pattern of shapes and planes, or was he interested in what lay beneath the surface?

As I tried to imagine what he was seeing, I became aware of the space around me in a different way. It was no longer empty, but charged with dancing particles, which left me feeling hollow. In a kind of protest, I shifted my attention to my body, the circulation of my blood, the weight of my limbs, and realized that they were beginning to feel cramped. To distract myself, I studied the corner of the room I could see. I couldn't read the titles of the books without my glasses, and there were no objects in the studio to give me further clues about its inhabitants. With some annoyance, I realized that I was looking for traces of the woman I had seen at the Fourth of July parade, and that I was relieved to discover none.

"Would you like to take a break and stretch?" His voice surprised me. I had dropped into a kind of dream state and become unaware of the passage of time. I stood up and stretched, suddenly feeling the ache in my legs.

"Can I look?"

"I never show unfinished work. What about a cup of tea?"

He put a kettle on the stove and lit a cigarette.

"Who was the lady who was gardening? She looked at me very suspiciously."

"Mrs. Holloway? She's a journalist. She lets me live here in exchange for being a kind of caretaker. She's a bit fierce, but she's actually a very fine investigative reporter. She did excellent pieces about PAVE PAWS and the nuclear plant in Plymouth."

"What on earth is PAVE PAWS?"

"You should ask her. It's some kind of high-powered radar—part of our early warning defense system. People like Mrs. Holloway suspect that being bombarded by all that radiation isn't doing us any good."

"You mean while we speak, we're being zapped by invisible rays?"

"Something like that. But don't worry, it's mostly the other end of the Cape that's getting it. And some of the side effects are benign—like more girl babies being born. There are so many other things that could cause an increase in cancer it's not worth thinking about."

"Are you making this up to make me feel bad?"

"Not at all. The Air Force, of course, denies everything, but you should really talk to Mrs. Holloway. Her reports on the near-accidents at the Plymouth plant will really brighten your day. I suspect your lovely sunsets are really caused by nuclear garbage."

Even if what he said was true, it seemed almost as if he took pleasure in painting this creepy picture of a world of unseen and sinister forces. I was wondering why he was doing it, and if I should leave, when Sean poured boiling water into the teapot. Suddenly the fresh smell of mint filled the studio, chasing out the unpleasant atmosphere. He handed me a cup.

"It's good," I said, surprised. Normally mint tea tastes like toothpaste to me.

"It's the way they make it in Morocco. You mix fresh mint with green tea."

Someone else had mentioned Morocco recently.

"Have you been there?" I asked, while I tried to remember who it was.

"Several times."

Then I remembered. Molly had said her mother wore a Moroccan scent.

"Did you know Maria, Molly's mother?" I asked abruptly.

"Yes, I knew her."

It was obvious that he didn't want to talk about Maria, and I felt as if I had been clumsy. I took another sip, but now the taste of the tea and the remembered scent seemed like an infusion of everything exotic that I had never experienced, and probably never would.

"I think I should go now," I said.

He looked at his watch. "Yes. I don't think I want to do any more tonight, and I don't think I want to continue with the sketch."

I hadn't realized until then that somehow or other I had hoped the sittings might continue. But obviously I had been found wanting.

"I think I'd like to attempt a painting. Do you think you could come back again tomorrow?"

"I guess so," I said, trying to conceal my feeling of reprieve. "Cheryl didn't seem to mind."

"Good. I'll see you tomorrow."

As I stepped outside, I found myself glad to breathe normal air, instead of the air inside the studio, which seemed charged with things I didn't understand. Then I remembered that it was probably filled with toxic waste of some sort or another.

"Never mind," I thought, and began walking home, irrationally lightened by the idea that I would return the next day.

This time I walked along Old Country Road. As I passed a neat cottage with blue shutters, a station wagon pulled into the driveway. Mabel got out and began unloading shopping bags.

"Let me help," I said, and grabbed two bags.

"Would you like to come in for a cup of tea?" she asked. What I could see of her kitchen looked cozy and inviting.

"I'd love to, but I should get back."

"Another time then."

It seemed to me she gave me a funny look, but there was no way she could have known where I had been.

CHAPTER TWLEVE

July 30th

I have not wanted to write for almost two weeks. Perhaps I am so unacquainted with happiness that I am afraid to name it. Afraid that it will vanish like fairy food.

Happiness. On the page, the word looks trite, like something on a greeting card. Perhaps it is not the right word after all for the time I spend with Sean, linked as it is in my mind with twilight and shadows and a feeling of uncertainty.

He has been working on the painting. We meet several times a week, but each time I wonder if he will want me back—fearing, I suppose, that he will get tired of the painting, or of me as a subject. He has refused to let me see it until it is finished. That seems strange to me, but so is he. Strange and moody. Sometimes he is friendly and cheerful, at other times distant and rather cold. Each time I turn up, I am not certain who will be waiting for me.

Mrs. Holloway watches my comings and goings with what I take to be a cold, journalistic eye. I have no idea whether her investigations include the human heart, or whether she speculates about my presence, or simply dislikes the intrusion. I feel she runs a very tight ship and likes to control her surroundings. I see it in her garden, so different from Maria's, which I imagine, even when she was alive, she allowed to riot and tangle, plants following their own inclinations. Mrs. Holloway's garden toes the line. She must follow a strict schedule, because when I turn up she is always there, pinching off dead heads and yanking out weeds. Her garden is filled with sturdy plants that know their place— marigolds and zinnias—the space between them well defined, the borders neat. I admire the care she puts into her garden, but it does not touch me in the way Maria's does, with its fragile woodsy flowers and touch of Victorian melancholy.

Sean and I have begun to talk a little during our tea break. I still see no sign of the woman at the parade, and I find that I both do and don't want to know more. Mostly I am happy to be adrift in time—not to think about the past or future. In one of our conversations, Sean told me about a book he once read about prisoners during the Second World War who invented a twenty-fifth hour in which they could be free. That's the way I feel about the time we spend together. A bit like Narnia time, which exists in its own dimension—years can pass in Narnia, but when you return, no time at all has elapsed.

Yesterday as I was gathering up the teacups to put them in the sink, I noticed a book on top of the shelf. On the cover was a scarecrow photographed against a dark sky, its tattered clothes blowing in the wind and its face partially collapsed. Something about the way it was photographed made it seem more like a totem than an ordinary scarecrow. The title of the book was *Ephemeral Art*, and the author was Maria Dyer.

"I didn't know she'd published a book," I said.

"Just this one. A small press in Boston."

I opened up the book. On the title page was written, "For Sean, another friend of short-lived phenomena, with love, Maria."

"What does that mean?"

"There's actually something called the Center for Short-Lived Phenomena in Cambridge. They study brief, inexplicable things, like a sudden rain of frogs in Burma, meteor showers…Maria loved that sort of thing, and the idea that there were serious scientists studying them."

I leafed through the book. The photographs were of sand sculptures, snowmen, scarecrows, jack-o'-lanterns, even some elaborately decorated cakes. The last photograph was of an immense funeral wreath, the flowers arranged in the shape of an angel. Without knowing anything about photography, it seemed to me that the photographs themselves were not as good as the ones in the house, but there was something poignant about the fact that nothing photographed in the book was meant to last—each subject would melt, be erased by the tides, rot, or be eaten. All of them were gone now, except for their images that Maria had frozen in time.

"When I arrived there were these funny papier mâché skeletons...." I began.

"They're Mexican," he interrupted, "from the Day of the Dead. Like Halloween, but closer to the original idea of a day to honor wandering souls."

"Cheryl thought they were morbid."

"She would. But among the recurring motifs in art are images of death to remind us to live our lives to the fullest. Maria loved the Mexican skeletons because they're so full of humor."

"She told Molly this story about Billingsgate. It seems she was obsessed with things being destroyed by time."

"And yet surviving in another way. Don't forget that."

"Is there really a legend about Billingsgate?"

"I never heard it from anyone but Maria. My father is a fisherman. We used to sail out to the ruins sometimes. As far as I know, it was a perfectly ordinary fishing village that was washed away by tides and erosion. I always suspected it was a story she made up to amuse Molly. A kind of rehash of Avalon and Shambhala."

"I know Avalon was the island where King Arthur went when he died, but I never heard of Shambhala."

"It's a Tibetan legend. About a hidden kingdom. Perhaps it has a geographical location, like Shangri-la, or maybe it's just a metaphor for a state of mind."

"Molly told me about it. She didn't remember the name."

"It's the sort of story Maria would have wanted to share with Molly. She had a real gift for seeing magic in ordinary things."

"I think I saw that in her photographs."

"She was good. Very good..." He trailed off, his face shadowed. Perhaps it was just the fading light that touched me with a feeling of gloominess.

"What happened?" I asked at last. It was the question I had not dared to ask in all this time.

"To Maria?"

"How did she die?" It sounded bold, but I was suddenly sick of all the mystery.

"She drowned."

"An accident?"

"I don't think I ever really wanted to know. They found her body washed up on the beach. Apparently she had gone for a swim that night. There was a full moon…She was an excellent swimmer, but the currents can be deceptive, even in the bay."

"Could it have been deliberate?"

"She didn't leave a note, if that's what you mean. But she was one of those people who never seem absolutely solid in the world. It made her a wonderful friend. She always brought a taste of something *other*…a kind of heightened sense of the transitory…"

"It doesn't quite sound like what you'd want in a mother."

"I think in the early years, Molly grounded her. It was the happiest I ever saw her. But who knows what else was going on. I never really understood her relationship with Molly's father, and I think she may have felt she'd reached a plateau in her work. As if she were copying herself and couldn't break through to whatever was next. Perhaps she went for a swim and when she felt a current pulling her, she just decided to go with it. It's the kind of thing she would do...."

"Yes..." I remembered the current I had felt the night of the phosphorescent creatures. I turned the book over. On the back was a photograph. In this one, Maria's hair was shorter, and I could see that there were some streaks of gray in it and lines around her eyes.

"She aged," I said, with a trace of disappointment, remembering the laughing picture on Molly's bureau.

Sean stubbed out his cigarette. "It will happen even to you...Nevertheless, she remained one of the most beautiful women I've ever met."

For the first time I wondered if Sean hadn't been a little bit in love with her. More even than the women in Provincetown, Maria was everything I was not. Beautiful. Talented. Mysterious... And dead, I added with a mixture of triumph and hopelessness. Because how can you ever compete with someone who will never be tarnished by real time?

"Would you like to go for a drive?"

His voice startled me. I had been lost in my

thoughts, and we had always remained in the studio. When he was finished painting, I left.

"There isn't much light left," he said, "and I don't really feel like painting anymore."

"I'd love to," I said, still surprised at the suggestion.

"Come on, then. I'll show you the dunes."

He put his hand on my shoulder to propel me through the door. I know it meant nothing. It's what I might do with Molly, but still, he had never touched me like that before.

As we climbed into the battered green Land Rover, I saw Mrs. Holloway watching us from her kitchen window.

I had never been in a Land Rover before. The springs were shot, so we lurched over every bump, and the car was so noisy it was difficult to talk, but it didn't matter. There was something exhilarating simply about being in this car, which objectively smelled of gasoline but to me had the smell of adventure.

We drove along Route 6 in the direction of Provincetown, but struck off into the dunes before we reached it. Once off the main road, the dunes really are like something out of *Lawrence of Arabia*—just right for this car. We wound through the dunes until we reached the ocean.

Sean drove down to the beach itself, and as we scrunched along the wet sand, the incoming waves occasionally splashed my door with spray. I thought that I had never been so happy in my life. Suddenly I called out, "Stop!"

Sean slammed on the brakes, nearly pitching me through the windshield. "What on earth?"

"Ahead of us. I think there's something in the tracks."

We had been following the tire tracks of previous vehicles. Ahead of us, caught in the deep rut made by another tire, was a baby bird. Above my head, two plovers piped frantically to each other. As I approached, the bird scurried ahead of me, a little animated ball of feathers. I blocked it with my hand and scooped it up. I could feel its heart thudding furiously as I cupped it in my hands. I brought it round to Sean's window.

"Look," I said. "Isn't it the most exquisite thing?"

I bent over it, my chin grazing the soft feathers. In a moment I would set it free again, but for this instant it seemed to me that I had captured the fragile essence of this evening.

I looked up and saw that he was looking at me instead of the bird with an expression I had not seen before.

"Don't change," he said.

"What?" I said, stupidly.

"Forget it," he said. "Of course you will. It's just that right now everything's so fresh for you. Like a blank canvas..."

I released the bird, and it scurried off hysterically.

As we watched the sun sink in silence, Sean became remote again. I found myself wondering what he was thinking, and why he had asked me to come with him.

CHAPTER THIRTEEN

August 7th

Things never stay the same. If I didn't suspect that already, it is the lesson I have learned from *All Our Days*. Characters meet, are attracted to each other, and overcome obstacles to be together. But the moment they embrace, you know it's the beginning of the end. Something will come between them, because if it didn't, there wouldn't be a story. I'm glad I'm not a soap opera writer. The very thought of all that endless flux makes me tired, but unfortunately it seems to me that this is the one aspect of the soaps that is true to life.

In a way, I envy the characters in *All Our Days*, who, despite their years of experience to the contrary, remain cheerfully unaware of the pitfalls their writers are plotting for them even as they say, "Nothing can come between us now!"

As I drove back from the dunes with Sean that night a week ago, it occurred to me that there would be a time when I would look back on that day as one with a special kind of happiness. I recognized that it marked a transition of sorts, after which things could either go forward, or not—and I didn't dare to imagine them going forward—toward what? Even with my meager experience, it seems to me that moments on the cusp, still full of possibility, are the most exciting.

Not that anything very dramatic has happened. The real trouble is that I don't seem to be able to tell if things are happening or not. Either with Sean or the house.

Whatever is or is not going on in the house, I feel I am partially to blame. I still put in my hours with Molly. We go to the beach or to the pond. Sometimes we go sailing in *Dawn Treader*. But I know I am as out of it as she is.

Molly's father called to say his shoot has been

extended because of bad weather. The contractors have finished with the bathrooms and begun in the dining room, putting in a large window with a curved top, and so many little panes it makes me dizzy. Outside, some painters have begun scraping the peeling shingles. Molly responds to it all impassively. I can only guess at her feelings, and don't pry. I spend my time waiting for the days I go to the studio—for those few hours when I feel myself coming alive. I yearn for twilight, and our odd conversations, whose spaces and silences I fill with meaning. Nothing, I repeat, has happened. And yet there are times when I feel something is different.

The other day, in the middle of a sitting, I felt a change in temperature. I can't find a better way to describe it. I became aware that something had shifted in the atmosphere. One moment Sean was looking at me as he always does—what I imagine as a pattern of shapes and colors—and the next he was looking at me in a different way. As if he were really seeing me. Our eyes met, as they don't often do. There was something in his look—perhaps assessing, perhaps containing a question—that was both exciting and frightening. As if the moment demanded something, but I had no idea what.

After a moment, he went back to painting again in the old way. But during our tea break, we had our first personal conversation. As we sipped our mint tea, he suddenly asked if I had a boyfriend back home. It seemed like such an intrusion into our special time that I was startled and merely shook my head.

"How come?"

"The boys my age are such geeks." He looked amused, and I was afraid I'd revealed myself too transparently. "What about you?" I asked quickly, because the conversation was making me nervous. "Who was the lady in the straw hat?"

"Linda? When did you ever see her?"

"At the Fourth of July parade."

"I didn't see you there. She's…a friend. She works as a stylist for a fashion photographer in New York—arranging the props and costumes and all that—and a bit freelance as an artist's rep."

"She's very pretty."

"She isn't, you know. She's extremely attractive. She has a lot of style and a great deal of energy. It's not the same thing at all."

"She's in New York now?"

"She's in the south of France, on a shoot. But I'm not actually sure she's coming back here."

"No?" I said, trying not to sound hopeful.

"We had a kind of fight. She has an idea that she'd like to give up her work and live here year-round. But she'd never last. She's one of those people who need to feel they're a part of what's happening. And believe me, nothing is happening here in the winter, unless you make it happen yourself. It's the shadow side of all the summer activity. Only someone with a strong inner life can make it—if they don't crack."

"That doesn't sound like a reason to fight, exactly."

"I'm afraid I called her a vampire. With all her energy, she still feeds on other people's talent. She took offense."

"I guess I can see how she could."

"I can be very offensive."

His tone was almost satisfied. But was it a challenge? A warning?

I don't think it's just my imagination that after that, something changed. I waited to see if he would ask me to go for another drive, but he didn't. It was as if in talking about ourselves, we had broken a tacit understanding and acknowledged a kind of vacuum that perhaps was better unacknowledged.

We all know how nature feels about vacuums. It seemed to me that this one was filled by an unexpected presence. I couldn't help thinking that when Sean talked about surviving the long dark winters, he was talking about Maria, who had pursued her work in a shadowy realm, but seemed, in the end, to have been claimed by her shadows.

As I was walking home, I noticed a blue station wagon parked by the side of the road. Mabel was inspecting some shrubs. She looked up as I came over to greet her.

"Just checking on these beach plums. Have a feeling they'll ripen early this year."

Nestled between the leaves were some little yellowish globes barely tinted with red. They looked hard and bitter.

"They don't look too edible right now," I said.

"Don't look it. But there's a lot going on inside them. Can't you feel it?"

I shook my head. They just looked like hard little lumps.

"There's always a lot of energy when something's turning into something else."

"You're not talking about beach plums," I said.

"It's all the same thing—the moment when day turns into night, summer into fall, childhood into adolescence.... It's the most exciting time, but it's also the most dangerous."

"Why?" I said. This conversation was making me nervous too, but I felt I had to ask.

"They're powerful times, transitions. What enters isn't always what you expect."

"Molly..." I began. But I knew she was also warning me for myself.

She patted me on the arm. "Don't look so

worried, honey. You have a lot of good sense. I'm not telling you anything you don't already know."

But as I walked back to the house, I wondered just how much good sense I had.

That was the night that things began to happen. It began with footsteps on my stairs. I woke with a start, out of a confused dream, to hear someone approaching my room.

"Molly?" I called out, thinking she might have had a bad dream. There was no answer. I waited for Tobermory to push open the door, although the steps sounded too heavy for a cat. The footsteps continued on the landing and then stopped outside my door. I could feel someone on the other side, waiting. Someone was concentrating—wondering whether or not to knock?

"Come in," I called. But there was no answer.

Unable to bear the suspense, I jumped out of bed and flung open the door. There was no one there, and yet I had not heard the footsteps descending. It must have been my overactive imagination, but I could almost have sworn that I smelled a trace of something that reminded me of furniture polish....

In the cold light of day, I decided that in my half-sleep, I had taken for footsteps the creaking of the stairs as the house settled, and imagined that I had smelled the scent.

I decided not to mention the incident to Molly. I remembered my conversation with Mabel, and decided Molly needed no further encouragement in that direction.

Molly and I try to leave the house as quickly as possible these days. The contractors have finally reached the old part of the house. They are sanding the lovely old wide-planked floors, and scraping the paint off the paneling above the fireplace. I must admit that the pine underneath is beautiful, and yet the way the men work seems invasive. The layers should be gently uncovered by a sympathetic hand, not zapped off with whirring machinery.

I didn't hear footsteps last night, but when I came downstairs this morning there was a minor scene. There were some smudgy marks that looked like footprints in the polyurethane, which had not quite dried on the living room floor and now had some sand and seaweed embedded in it. Cheryl was accusing Molly of having done the mischief, and Molly was denying it, pointing out that her feet were smaller that the prints.

"What do you suggest, then? That it was Tobermory, or Julia?" I thought I caught her sneaking a look at my feet, which in this case I am happy to say are quite enormous—much bigger than the smudges.

"I had nothing to do with it. It isn't the sort of thing I would do."

As a matter of fact, it seemed to me exactly the sort of thing she *would* do, but she was so defiant, and so near tears, that I found myself believing her. Besides, I have always found her to be a very truthful child.

I waited until we were down at the beach and then asked, "Well, did you do it?"

"I swear I didn't. Cross my heart and hope to die."

"You don't have to go that far. And frankly I don't care if you did. I'd understand it if you had. But it's important you tell me the truth—for my own sanity."

And then I told her about the footsteps.

"I heard them too," she said. "They came into my room."

"They did?"

"Of course. I told you my mother wouldn't let them destroy the house."

"You don't really believe that."

"I smelled her perfume."

"But you haven't seen her," I said, trying to maintain my grasp on things.

"No. But her walk was very distinctive. So was her scent."

"She can't possibly win," I said, realizing I was entering Molly's reality. "Cheryl is very determined."

"You didn't know my mother."

We both looked up as the sound of a plane

shattered the quiet of the beach. A yellow biplane flew low across the water, towing a banner. As the wind pulled it out straight, we read, HAPPY SWEET SIXTEEN, ASHLEY. We looked at each other in disgust.

"How gross," said Molly.

"It must have cost a fortune to hire a plane like that."

"That doesn't mean anything to them. They're having a clambake tonight to celebrate. We're all invited."

"I didn't know."

"You don't know much about what's happening at the house anymore."

It was the first time she'd expressed any bitterness at my desertion.

"I'm not sure I can come," I began.

"Too busy with Sean?"

"What makes you think I see him?"

"I know a lot more than anyone thinks I do."

"What do you think I am, dumb or something?" we both said at the same time, and then laughed and linked pinkies.

"What goes up the chimney?" I asked Molly

"Smoke."

"May your wish and my wish never be broke."

There was something reassuring about the childish ritual, but I wondered what Molly had wished, and did not dare to name my own wish even to myself.

Chapter Fourteen

When I arrived at Sean's, there was no sign of the green Land Rover. I knocked at the door anyway, but there was no answer. As usual, Mrs. Holloway was yanking out some microscopic weeds.

"Do you know when Sean will be back?" I asked her.

"Sean and I keep to ourselves. Was he expecting you?"

"I thought so."

"I'm just about to go inside. The mosquitoes are vicious tonight. Why don't you come in and wait?"

Surprised at the invitation, I followed her inside. The kitchen was unexpected. I hadn't imagined fierce Mrs. Holloway as a cook, but on the shelves was a nice jumble of old mixing bowls and pots, and the worn pine table had obviously seen a great many meals. Mrs. Holloway poured herself a glass of white wine, and when she offered me one too, I didn't refuse as I normally would.

"Sean's never missed an appointment before," I said.

She looked at me appraisingly. It was the first time I had seen her without her hat. Her gray hair was cut in a bob, and her blue eyes, though sharp, were not unkind.

"If this is the first time you've been disappointed, you're fortunate."

"I'm not disappointed," I said quickly. "It's just that I thought we had an appointment for a sitting."

"Yes, of course. Just a word of warning, my dear. You're very young"—I was sick of being told that, all right—"and men like Sean can do a great deal of damage. Perhaps without meaning to. Or perhaps they don't care."

"I'm just sitting for him."

"I understand. But you're at a vulnerable age, and men like Sean can be dangerously seductive."

"It's not like that at all," I began, wondering why she was telling me all this, and trying to imagine shrewd Mrs. Holloway as ever having been vulnerable, but she interrupted me.

"I hope you don't think I'm giving you advice about your body when I don't even know you. I'm talking about something much more dangerous—a seduction of the spirit—an implied promise of something men like Sean can never deliver, but that will make you despise what is available to you. Just a friendly warning, my dear."

"Thank you," I said stiffly. I could feel the unaccustomed alcohol beginning to make things a bit fuzzy. Partly out of curiosity, and partly to avoid any more unsolicited advice, I asked, "Did you know Maria Hayes?"

"We all know each other here. Although I didn't know her well. She and I didn't have a great deal in common."

"How do you mean?"

"She had talent, of a sort. And a certain charm—at least others seemed to think so"—I wondered if she was thinking about Sean—"but she was one of those people who never seem to come to terms with things as they are."

"Is that so bad?"

"For one thing, it meant that while you were with her, you felt she was never really there. And I think it killed her in the end."

"What do you mean?"

"I don't believe for one moment that her death was an accident, whatever they may say."

"Why?"

I remembered that she was an investigative reporter. Perhaps I would finally learn some hard facts. But as if she guessed my thoughts, she said, "Oh I don't know any of the details, about how and where she was found. But I always felt she was one of those people who couldn't accept her own aging. Or the fact that her own work wasn't going anywhere."

"Yes, I see." I took another sip of my wine. Either it or the conversation was beginning to make me feel slightly sick.

"Some people," she continued, "have a strong attraction to the unknown. They seem drawn by shadows. It's another kind of seduction. It's been called the Lure of Faery. But it can turn into a love of death."

I had finished the rest of my wine, and I realized I didn't want to hear any more of what Mrs. Holloway had to say. There was something strong in Maria's work, which I refused to see just as something negative. "Thank you for the wine," I said. "I don't think I'll wait any longer for Sean."

"A wise move," said Mrs. Holloway, and poured herself another glass of wine. As I started to walk back home, I wondered who had once hurt Mrs. Holloway so badly.

The house was empty when I got back. Then I remembered the clambake. I was feeling a bit light-headed, and perhaps because I didn't want to be left alone with my thoughts, I walked down to the beach.

They had dug a huge pit and filled it with hot rocks and seaweed. Buried in the mound were lobsters, clams, and corn on the cob, which had been steaming for hours. Young men in white jackets had organized it and were now doing the serving. I had the feeling that it all came under Molly's idea of vulgarity, but I had to admit that it smelled delicious. One of the young men handed me a plate of steamed clams, and they tasted just as good as they smelled.

I spotted Molly sitting at the edge of the party, rather grimly gnawing on an ear of corn. On my way over to her, I passed Ashley, sitting among a group of kids I imagined were the Yacht Club crew, and wished her a happy birthday. Todd was sitting with her, next to a boy with sandy-colored hair and horn-rimmed glasses perched on a beaky nose.

I was surprised when Todd greeted me, "Hi. You're looking nice tonight."

I was still wearing my outfit for the painting. It was the first time he had ever seen me with my hair out and without my glasses.

"This is my friend, Paul," he said, introducing beaky nose. "He's at school with me and is just starting as an intern at the Center for Coastal Studies."

"That must be interesting," I said, and started to move on.

"Don't you want to join us?" asked Todd.

"Molly looks a little lost. I think I'll join her."

"Suit yourself."

I made my way over to Molly.

"What are you doing here?" she asked. Her tone wasn't too friendly, but I thought she looked pleased to see me.

"Change of plans," I said, and dunked a clam in melted butter. For a few moments we ate silently. It's hard to maintain a conversation and eat corn and steamers at the same time.

"Mind if I join you?" It was Todd's friend Paul, carrying two paper plates with lobster and corn on them. He handed me one. "I brought you this."

"Thanks. What about your friends?"

"Oh, they're not my friends. Except for Todd. I got a bit tired of listening to them gossip about people I don't know."

"I know what you mean." I excavated a piece of lobster from its shell. It was wonderful, with a taste of seaweed and a smoky taste from the fire. "I feel a bit rotten eating their food. Molly and I were putting down the whole event this morning."

"Collaborating with the enemy?"

I laughed. "I guess so. But I thought you were…"

"One of them?"

"Something like that."

"Not really. Todd's really okay, you know. He can't help his parents. I'm on scholarship at our school—just so you don't think I'm a rich kid."

"What is this Center for Coastal Studies?"

"It's in Provincetown. Most of their work now has to do with whales."

"What do you do there?"

"We go out on the whale watch ships. It's a tourist thing, but we're able to collect a lot of data on the whales. We have files on almost five hundred individuals. We identify them by their markings and keep records of their activity, the number of calves…things like that. I spend most of my time back in the lab, helping to organize the data. But the best part is when I get to go out on the ships."

"I've never seen a whale close up."

"No matter how many times I have, it's still thrilling."

"How close do you get?"

"Sometimes several yards. They don't seem to mind the boats. Sometimes they'll do a kind of display—beating the water with their flippers, or breaching. No one is sure what it all means, but it's very dramatic."

"It sounds neat. I'd love to see it."

"Why don't you come out on the boat some time?"

"I'd like that."

"I'll try to arrange it."

Shortly afterward, we were called back to the group for the cutting of the cake. It was enormous, shaped like a heart, with sixteen candles. I wondered if Maria would have thought it worthy of photographing. Ashley closed her eyes and made a wish. As she blew out the candles, her face caught their glow. I felt a pang of envy. Whatever she wished for was probably very clear and within her grasp. I thought that probably it was not the sort of picture Maria took.

Paul sat beside me as the group gathered around the remains of the fire and began to sing. I didn't join in. I never do. And neither did he. I was aware of his presence by my side. He seemed interesting and easy to talk to. He even seemed to like me. If I went out on the whale watch boat, I would probably have a good time....But I could feel my thoughts pulled out to the darkness that had settled over the bay. Where was Sean, and why hadn't he been home? And why were my thoughts still turning in his direction?

CHAPTER FIFTEEN

August 8th

This morning I vowed I wouldn't go to Sean's. All day I thought about how I wasn't going to go, but as seven o'clock rolled around, I found myself being pulled toward Mrs. Holloway's. Instead, I joined Molly and Cheryl as they watched *All Our Days.* Cheryl said she was happy I was going to watch this episode because she had a lot of fun writing it. I waited to see what she thought was fun.

At first I was struck by how little had happened since I had last watched. Lila had finally discovered she was pregnant, but Lance was still being torn between her and Sandi. I had this sense of time being very elastic—hours stretching over days, and days over weeks, as the writers struggled to fill up episodes. It struck me that *All Our Days* is the exact opposite of what I myself think is romantic, which is a heightening and condensing of reality instead of this taffylike stretching out of the most everyday events. I was just thinking how accurate the title was—"not *all* our days, please"—when the episode was interrupted by a kind of dream sequence.

Lance, who has committed himself to Lila because he believes he is the father of her child, meets Sandi by accident and sees her as Catherine in *Wuthering Heights,* and Sandi sees him as Heathcliff. The sequence was filmed in black-and-white, and the actors were wearing costumes that looked like those in the old movie.

I was speechless. Didn't Cheryl realize how embarrassing it was to compare these pieces of plastic to those characters? And then I felt queasy. I usually try not to examine my own imaginings, but are they really any less ridiculous?

Afterward, to rid myself of my crummy feeling, I asked Molly if she would like me to read to her. We long ago finished *The Lion, the Witch and the Wardrobe,* and now she was close to the end of *Voyage of the Dawn Treader.* I could feel my voice beginning to catch as Reepicheep, the gallant mouse, set out alone for Aslan's country. By the time Lucy and Edmund were told they could never return to Narnia, tears were trickling down my cheeks. As I closed the book, I saw Molly watching me, dry-eyed.

"It's all right," she said. "My mother cried too. But remember, Aslan tells them the door into his country is from our own world."

"It's just a book, Molly."

"That's not what my mother said."

I didn't feel like giving her a lecture on allegory, or Christian propaganda. I remembered that I'd felt a bit cheated myself when I figured out Aslan's other name, and there was no denying that the book still left me with a feeling of yearning.

"Go to sleep," I said, "and dream of Narnia. Perhaps that's one of the ways in."

As I started downstairs, I head the phone ring. I waited for Cheryl to answer it, but when she didn't, I picked up the receiver.

"Hello," I said.

There was no answer, but on the open line, I heard what sounded like waves breaking.

"Hello," I said again. "Is anyone there?"

The only response was the sighing of the wind, but I could feel a presence at the other end of the phone, waiting and listening, as it had waited and listened at the other side of my door.

"Who is it?" I asked. "What do you want?"

There was something unnerving about the inhuman sounds on the other end—a sense of emptiness and loneliness....I banged down the receiver.

Back in my room, I knew I couldn't sleep. I sat there and thought about the mysterious phone call, and about why Sean hadn't been there for the sitting. I thought about my feelings for Sean, and Molly's feeling about Billingsgate, and decided that Cheryl is probably the only sane person in the house. She's the only one whose head isn't filled with impossible imaginings and who has the sense to use other people's dreams to make a fortune....

The more I thought about things, the worse I felt. Finally I decided to walk down to the beach.

It was well after the time Sean painted there, so I didn't think it broke my vow.

It had been a long time since I had been down to the bay alone after dark. The fireflies were now gone, and the sky was overcast. The bright outside lamps of the new houses cast garish slashes of light across the road. So much for magic.

The night air was damp and clinging. Instead of walking down to the beach, I sat at the top of the stairs. The lights of Provincetown were obscured by the haze, and I turned in the other direction, toward Billingsgate. Here too, haze reduced the horizon and shoreline to a murky blur. I concentrated, trying to probe the darkness. I was still unsettled by the phone call, but I could not detect anything out there that corresponded to what I had felt at the other end of the phone. It must have been a wrong number, nothing more....

With a jolt I noticed the silhouette of a man walking along the beach toward the steps. There was no tell-tale glow of a cigarette, but his shape was tall and thin and he was wearing a bulky jacket. No one else I knew walked on the beach at night.

I was trying to decide what I was going to say when the figure approached the foot of the stairs. He looked up and the light from one of the houses on the dunes slanted across sandy hair and glasses.

I watched as Paul climbed the steps. I knew it was totally unfair, but I found myself hating him simply for being who he was—and myself for having hoped for a minute that he was somebody else.

"Hi there," he said. "Do you come here often?"

"Only when I want to be by myself." It came out sounding nastier than I had intended, but he disregarded my tone.

"Me too. There's a killer Ping-Pong game going on back at the house. I wasn't in the mood."

He sat down on the steps, and for a while we both stared out at the bay.

"What do you think the whales are doing right now?" I asked at last, because the silence was beginning to get on my nerves.

"I've never been out at night, but I don't think they do anything too different. They're voluntary breathers, so they'd drown if they really went to sleep underwater. From time to time they just rest for about fifteen minutes, floating on the surface. It's called 'logging.'"

"That seems sad somehow—like mammals ought to be able to dream."

"Who says they don't? Maybe it's all a kind of dreamtime to them. It's one of the things about our research. We accumulate masses of statistics, but there's so much we'll probably never know."

"Doesn't that bother you?"

"I like the idea of chipping away at the de-tails—kind of like a jigsaw puzzle. You start with the bits that have straight edges, and then the bits that fit into those, and gradually the big space in the center begins to shrink…"

"I have to get back," I said, standing up abruptly.

"Oh, okay." He looked surprised. There was no way of explaining to him that I was actually in danger of enjoying the conversation.

We walked down the road together in silence. I was trying to figure out why I had cut short a conversation I was finding interesting, and I suppose he was trying to figure out why I was so weird.

When we got to the driveway, he hesitated as if he were going to ask me something. But all he said was, "See you around."

As I opened the door to the kitchen, I heard Tobermory meow. It wasn't his hunger meow, or the indignant sound he makes when Lucy tries to chew his tail. It was his chirp of greeting, which I've only heard him make when he jumps on Molly's bed, and when he saw Mabel. I decided Molly hadn't been able to sleep either and had come down to the kitchen for a snack.

The kitchen was deserted, except for Tobermory, who crouched by his dish, staring at the open door. As I watched, he meowed again and walked toward the dining room. I followed him slowly and stopped on the threshold.

Tobermory was standing in the middle of the room, rubbing against something that wasn't there. That, of course, made no sense. He must have an itch, or something, but it certainly looked as if he were rubbing his head against an invisible leg. And if he had an itch, why could I hear him purring from where I stood?

My heart and my skin began doing all the stupid things you usually read about in bad descriptions. Obviously the animals in the house were now as crazy as the rest of us. I suppose Tobermory was entitled to greet an imaginary friend.... Nevertheless, I remained rooted on the spot. The dining room still smelled of new paint. Surely it was my imagination that I thought I detected another scent beneath it.

The spell was broken by a sound from upstairs—what sounded like a stealthy footfall. Tobermory stopped purring and looked up. Annoyed, because I had really been quite frightened, I marched upstairs to see what was going on.

It was quiet now, but there was a crack of light around the locked door. Without giving myself a chance to think, I pulled on the knob and the door flew open.

Molly was sitting at a desk in a small room. Above the desk was a bulletin board with photographs tacked to it. The only other furniture in the room was a wicker chair and a bookcase crammed with books. From one corner of the bulletin board, several sheets of contact prints hung by a clip.

"What are you doing here?" I demanded, to mask how frightened I had been.

"What are *you* doing here?" she retorted. "Don't you know you're supposed to knock?"

"This room has always been locked. Why?"

"It was my mother's study. She turned the bathroom into a darkroom."

"But why was it locked?"

"Cheryl didn't like my coming here. She thought it was morbid. She didn't know I had a key."

"Cheryl was right."

I don't know why I said it, except that I was on edge, and I was sick of being frightened, sick of Maria and shadow worlds and things I didn't understand.

"Your mother's dead," I said. "It's creepy to pretend she's still around."

"Pretend!" said Molly. "I'm not the one who pretends. It's you who imagines things, about Sean and who knows what else. Get out!"

"I won't," I said. "I'm supposed to be looking after you. I won't leave until you come with me."

I hadn't realized we were both shouting until

Cheryl opened the door in yet another flouncy peignoir.

"What's going on?" she demanded. "And why are you in this room, Molly?"

Molly glared back at her.

"That's it," said Cheryl. "I believe I told you I didn't want you in this room. For your own good. But you wouldn't listen to me. From the day I walked into this house I've tried—and you've continued to treat me like an enemy. I've had enough. Tomorrow we begin on this room."

I gasped, but Molly remained icily calm. She picked up Lucy and started out of the room. As she passed me she hissed, "I hate you."

I am back in my room now, even less able to sleep. I feel terrible about betraying Molly. My only excuse is that I'm frightened. I admit it. And confused. I don't know what's going on.

It's no consolation that I've just remembered another literary governess. One I forgot at the beginning of the summer—the narrator of *The Turn of the Screw*! We read it this year in English, and the teacher pointed out that Henry James is really tricky—it's never clear whether anyone else sees the ghosts. Can there be something in me that's connecting with something in the house? Or something left unfinished by Maria?

Books are one thing. Personally, I'm all for ghosts on the printed page. But do I honestly believe that Maria is moving among us?

I don't know. I do know that strange things are happening. And I know that I am not the only one to observe them. Molly says she heard footsteps, too. But I don't know how much to believe what she says. There seems to be tangible evidence...unless Molly is faking it.

Sitting here alone, I am trying to examine my feelings as honestly as I can. I'm frightened, because I'm up against something I don't understand. But am I also a little jealous? It's a strange reaction, but I can't imagine my own mother caring enough to come back in this way....

CHAPTER SIXTEEN

August 10th

Later that night, I crept into Molly's room to apologize, but she pretended to be asleep and wouldn't answer me.

When I came downstairs the next morning, Molly was opening the container of wax worms. She had a fresh scrubbed look and her hair was shiny, as if she had just washed it.

Molly didn't look up as I entered the kitchen.

"Hi," I said.

"Hi," she replied in a neutral voice, still without looking up.

"Look, Molly," I said. "I'm sorry about last night."

"It's all right," she said, as Lucy sucked up a wax worm.

"It's not all right. I lost it because I was upset—about something else. And now the room is going to be destroyed."

"It doesn't matter," said Molly in the same neutral voice. "It's just a room."

"Of course it matters," I said. "It's not just a room. It was special to your mother."

Molly looked at me at last. "Julia," she said very patiently, as if she were lecturing a backward child. "You don't understand. It doesn't matter. I don't need it anymore."

I'm not sure why this sentence, which ought to have reassured me, gave me the creeps more than anything that had happened the night before.

"Friends?" I asked, because I didn't know what else to say.

"Friends," she replied. But I was left with the feeling that she was humoring me.

"What shall we do today?" I asked.

"I need some new crayons. Let's bike into Wellfleet."

"Okay." I was glad for a specific mission, and

one that would surround me with other people. "I'd just like to shower first." Normally I used my bathtub with the clawed feet, but this morning I hoped that a shower might wash away some of my feeling of weirdness, so I went upstairs to the bathroom Molly and Cheryl shared.

I washed my hair and let the hot water pour over my head for a long time. When I got out of the shower, I felt a bit better. Until I looked at the bathroom mirror. Traced in its steamy surface were faint, wavery letters. They were hard to read because of the drips, but at last I made out "BLUE MOON."

I stared at them for a moment and then tramped downstairs.

"Did you write on the bathroom mirror?" I demanded.

"What are you talking about?" said Molly. "I've been down here the whole time."

It was true that I hadn't heard anyone come in, but the shower was noisy. Or she could have written on the mirror when she washed her hair this morning, and the letters would have appeared when it steamed up again.

"It's not funny," I said.

"I don't know what you're talking about."

"There's writing on the bathroom mirror. When I got out of the shower, someone had scribbled 'BLUE MOON' in the steam." Was it my imagination or had a secretive look come over her face? "What does that mean?"

"I have no idea."

"Yes you do!" I realized I was shouting and lowered my voice. "Yes you do, Molly. You told me yourself. It was part of the Billingsgate story."

"You ought to get a grip on yourself, Julia," she said maddeningly. "Maybe you ought to go back and see Sean. You seem to be getting very edgy."

I could feel myself about to scream, which would only prove her point, so I said, "Let's go into town if we're going," in the calmest voice I could manage.

We browsed around Wellfleet for a while, looking in the shops. The first *sale* signs had appeared in some of the stores. They gave me a start, because although it was still early August they heralded the end of the season. Afterward we biked to the pond in the woods, and by the time we returned, it was late afternoon.

The door to Maria's study was open, and everything had been cleared out of it. Molly glanced at it in silence and continued to her own room but I was left with a sick feeling.

Dinner was unnervingly civil. Both Cheryl and Molly made an effort to be pleasant to each other, which left me feeling that the undercurrents in the house were about to send me round the bend.

"I think I'll go for a walk," I said after dinner.

Molly looked at me meaningfully, but in fact I had no intention of visiting Sean. His shadowy world was the last thing I wanted at the moment. During dinner it had occurred to me that there was only one person I really wanted to see. One person whose warmth and common sense might help me sort out what I was feeling. One person who knew everyone involved. More than anything, I wanted to sit in Mabel's kitchen, eat something she had baked, and pour out my heart.

When I got to her cottage, her car was gone

and there was only one light on, the kind you leave on if you're not going to be home until late. I knocked anyway, but there was no answer. My feeling of disappointment was overwhelming, and I stood in the road, wondering what to do now.

My thoughts were interrupted by the loud sputtering of some vehicle. A motor scooter came around the bend, punctuated by backfiring. The driver, unrecognizable in a crash helmet, pulled it to a stop beside me, and I saw Paul's nose and glasses poking out from beneath the helmet.

"We have to stop meeting like this," he said.

I wasn't in the mood for either humor or company. When I didn't say anything, he continued, "I'm just going to the Dari Burger for some ice cream. Want to come?"

"No thanks." I wondered if I might have been tempted if he were on a Harley Davidson instead of a little scooter, and if the crash helmet didn't look so stupid.

"Another time then." He kicked the scooter into life, and in a moment he had disappeared over the top of the hill. As I listened to the sound of backfires receding into the distance, I thought it might have been fun to ride on a motor scooter at night. I wondered what it was in me that preferred clinging to my black mood, and what I was going to do next.

Once again it was my feet that made the decision for me. I found them taking one step after another in the direction of Mrs. Holloway's. After all, I was almost there.

I was half hoping that he wouldn't be there, but the fates are capricious. Or perhaps I hadn't sent very clear signals because I didn't know myself what I wanted.

He was sitting at the dining room table, bent over a book. He looked up when I knocked.

"Where have you been?" he asked.

"Where were you?" I replied, intelligently.

"You'd better come in," he said, and poured me a cup of tea without asking.

"I came the other day," I said. "You weren't here."

"That's true," he said.

I waited for an explanation, but one didn't appear to be forthcoming.

"Mrs. Holloway told me you were unreliable," I said.

"You've been discussing me with Mrs. Holloway?"

"I asked her if she knew when you'd be back."

"And she volunteered this advice. How thoughtful of her.... She happens to be right. I'm not reliable."

"It doesn't matter."

"Of course it matters. I'm not going to explain where I was, because that part of it doesn't concern you. But I've come to think these sittings aren't a good idea."

My face must have registered my feelings because he went on, "That's just it. I'm not a good person for you to be spending a lot of time with. You should be with kids your own age. Having a good time."

"I don't like kids my own age. I don't like having a good time."

"You see what I mean? That's complete rubbish."

"I don't mean I don't like having a good time.

I mean I don't like their idea of having a good time. I like coming here."

"That's my point, Julia. I'm not a nice person."

"I don't care."

"You should care."

"You're nice to me."

"I'm not. You're so damn trusting. Hasn't it ever occurred to you that I might be using you?"

I couldn't help it. Probably it was a sleepless night and all the weirdness at the house, but I found my eyes beginning to fill with tears.

"Julia…" He stood up, and I thought maybe he was going to come around the table to me, but instead he turned away and lit a cigarette. When he turned back, he said, "I've come to like our time together too. But I meant it when I said I wasn't a nice person. Now I'm trying to be nice. I don't want to hurt you."

"Can't we just continue as we were? There isn't that much of the summer left, and the painting is almost finished…"

"Things don't 'just continue.' Haven't you learned that yet?"

"Yes," I said. "I think I have. But I'd like to... continue with the sittings."

Our eyes met. Once again I couldn't read his expression, but I allowed myself to meet his gaze. He looked away first.

"What am I going to do with you?" he said, to no one in particular. Then, abruptly, "There's no light left anyway. Let's go for a walk."

Once again, he put his hand on my shoulder, as if to propel me out the door, but dropped it immediately.

Shadows had overtaken the studio, but outside the sky was still translucent with last light. Instead of heading down to the beach, as I had expected, he cut across Old County Road to a sandy road that led through the woods.

"It looks like the road that leads to the cemetery," I said.

"It is. There are several. It's one of the other good places at twilight. Do you mind?"

"I like it there," I said. But I wondered why he had chosen it tonight.

As we moved among the rustling trees, once again we were enveloped by shadow. A bird that I could not identify called out to another. Away from the light, it was cold and I shivered.

"Do you want to go back?"

I shook my head.

"Here." He took off his army jacket and helped me into it. His hand remained resting lightly on my shoulders. We continued to walk with our bodies barely touching. I was aware of his smell—nicotine and turpentine—and wondered, "If I look up now, will he kiss me?" I waited, content just to walk beside him. When I finally looked up, he was looking away.

After a minute, he dropped his arm. Darkness was descending rapidly. It was no longer the long twilight of early summer, and the evening chill contained a taste of fall—like the spring equinox when it seemed to me I could feel the flux of the seasons, but now it was the cold winter that lay ahead.

For the first time in the woods, I thought about the young women who had come here with the man from Provincetown who murdered them. Had they too been filled with a vague feeling of anticipation? Every one said the murderer was very nice. No one said that about Sean. Including Sean.... I wondered what would happen when we reached the cemetery....

What happened was that Sean lit a cigarette and I said, "Why do you smoke so much?"

Of all the stupid things I might have said, that may have been the stupidest. Certainly it broke whatever mood there was.

I asked myself afterward why I had chosen that particular moment to ask what was certain to be an annoying question. All I can say is that sometimes for someone pretty smart, I can be really dumb.

Sean stubbed out his cigarette. "I told you it was a filthy habit. Let's go back."

We walked back in silence. This time he didn't put his arm around me. "There will be another time," I thought. But I know, somehow, that's not the way things work.

Back at the studio, I started to take off his jacket.

"Why don't you keep it until tomorrow?" he said.

"Tomorrow?" I said.

"You're right. It would be a shame not to finish the painting. There isn't much time left."

It was cold back in the house. At least it felt so to me. As if it too had absorbed the chill of early autumn. And so I slept in the army jacket and the smell of nicotine and turpentine filtered through my dreams.

When I woke this morning, the jacket was clutched tightly around me. I had the feeling that some time in the future I would remember this night, and I thought, perhaps this is as close as you ever get to having your dream within your grasp.

Chapter Seventeen

I gave Sean his jacket back tonight. The sitting was businesslike and we talked very little. Last night I was elated that the sittings would continue, but today in the studio I felt a kind of flatness. Sean seems distant again, and I'm still not sure about what did or didn't happen in the cemetery.

As I walked home after the sitting, I noticed how much darker it was. The sky was already crowded with bright stars. If someone had been with me, I would have felt obliged to comment on how beautiful they were, but the fact was they seemed cold and remote—more like a winter sky. And I didn't want to think about the winter. From the top of the hill, I could see the lights of

Provincetown. The thought of people crowded in bars and restaurants, laughing with their friends, made me feel even more alone.

Just as I was approaching the house, I heard a loud thud and thought I saw a dark shape scuttling into the shadows. Neglected by Molly and me, the raccoons were at it again with a vengeance. The garbage pail was tipped over and leftover spaghetti was spread over the lawn, mixed with eggshells and old orange peels.

I was in no mood to start messing with slimy garbage and was about to continue into the house, when something caught my eye. Beneath some crumpled pages from *All Our Days* was something that looked like photo contact sheets. I picked them up and carried them into the kitchen.

The thirty-five millimeter frames were small, the size of large postage stamps, and I held them to the light to see them better. Most of the pictures were of Molly as a baby. I don't know what I was expecting, but the photos were disappointing. The sort of snapshots anyone might take of their baby. There were four sheets clipped together.

In the middle of the last sheet was one photo of someone else. A girl, or woman, with long dark hair. I looked closer. Was it Maria herself, taken in a mirror or something? And then I looked again. The girl was wearing round glasses. It was really hard to see detail in the small photo—and of course, what I thought was impossible—but I could almost have sworn that it was a photograph of myself....

I slammed the contact sheets down on the counter. I didn't want to look at the photo more closely. Obviously I'm not the only person in the world with dark hair and round glasses. A lot of people could look similar in that size photo....

Up in my room, I tried to read, but after a few minutes I knew that I couldn't concentrate. I was haunted by the image of the dark-haired girl on the contact sheet. With a sick feeling I realized that in some way it didn't matter whether or not it was really me. The fact that I'd even considered the possibility meant I acknowledged that I too had some spooky connection with Maria.

Suddenly, I wished I had someone to talk to. It was too late to drop in on Mabel, and what I wanted to ask her wasn't the kind of thing you asked on the phone.

On impulse, I went down to the phone in the kitchen and dialed quickly, before I could think twice. The phone rang four times, and then my mother's voice came on.

"I'm sorry I can't come to the phone right now, but please leave a message after the beep and I'll phone you right back."

I hung up before the beep. What I wanted from her, she probably couldn't give me. As I started up to my room, I wondered where she was and what she was doing.

At the foot of the stairs, I realized I wasn't ready to go up to my little room, where thoughts chased around in my head like squirrels. Through the open window, I could smell the heady scent of phlox from the garden. I opened the door and stepped out again into the night.

In the moonlight, the flowers in Maria's garden gleamed pale, their colors washed out by the silver light. Above me, the stars still seemed cold and distant, but the night seemed to intensify the scents of the garden—not only the sweet-smelling phlox, but a warm, earthy smell from the ground itself. The soil must have retained the heat of the day, because in the garden there was still a feeling of warmth. For the first time all day, I felt a sense of calm. Whatever changes had taken place in the house, Maria's flowers were still going about their business, growing as she had intended them to. For a moment, all my confused feelings about Sean dropped away and I found myself thinking about this woman whom I had never known, scattering seeds in the ground so many years ago....

And then I realized that there was something odd about the feeling of warmth in the garden. I had been cold walking back from Sean's. Why should the ground be warmer here than anywhere else? Slowly, I became aware of another presence.

"Tobermory?" I called out hopefully.

The feeling of being watched intensified, but no cat appeared.

"What do you want from me?" I whispered.

The next minute, I had bolted back into the kitchen and slammed the door—because the question had been addressed to Maria.

Back in my room, I thought again about the

photograph, which might or might not be me. No matter how I looked at it, I could not shake the feeling that whatever was going on, I was a part of it too.

I was just about to climb into bed again when it seemed to me I caught a movement outside. I reached the window in time to see a small figure in a white nightgown quietly open the kitchen door and slip inside. As I opened the door to my room, I could just make out the sound of bare feet tiptoeing in the kitchen. I knew I ought to go down there and find out where Molly had been, but I stood there on the landing for a count of ten, and then I went back into my room.

The presence I felt in the garden must have been Molly. She too must have gone out into the night and hidden when I came out. Obviously, I should find out what she was doing in the garden.

But I already know the answer. What I felt in the garden wasn't just Molly. In some way that I don't want to think about, I believe that Maria was there too.

That's why Molly seemed so calm about the destruction of the house and Maria's studio. She doesn't care because she really doesn't need them anymore. My responsibility is clear. I should go up to her room right now and have a long talk with her.

But here I still am, sitting on my bed and writing.

What does she need me for, anyway? She has her mother.

CHAPTER EIGHTEEN

August 11th

This morning everything seemed as bright as if it had been drawn with a set of kid's crayons. Molly was up before me, eating her cereal. Framed by the cow weather vane and copper pots, she looked like a little girl in a commercial—except that she was holding Lucy, who had a wax worm dangling from her mouth. If I hadn't seen her last night, it would never have occurred to me that she was concealing anything. In the bright kitchen it seemed crazy to imagine that she was somehow meeting her dead mother. Like me, she must have slipped outside for some air. I put water on for tea and knew that I wasn't going to ask her where she had been.

When I arrived at Sean's this evening, he was still distant. I'd been thinking of telling him about the photograph and about seeing Molly in the garden, but when I saw the set look on his face, I changed my mind.

I'd give anything to be able to turn back the clock to the evening we saw the plovers on the beach. Even in the moment, I'd known that particular feeling of joy doesn't last, and yet I don't understand why he has changed.

As he prepared his brushes, I glanced around the room, which has become so familiar. On top of the bookshelf was a pile of mail. Sticking out of it was the corner of an air mail envelope with red and blue stripes. Somehow, I was certain it was from Linda.

Usually I like the sound of the paint squishing on the canvas—there's something soothing and intimate about it—but today it got on my nerves. Whatever Sean was painting, I knew he wasn't thinking about me. I guessed he was thinking about Linda and what was in the letter. How could

I ever have imagined that Sean could find me the least bit interesting when he knows someone glamorous like that?

One of the things that has made the sittings special for me is being alone with Sean in this space removed from ordinary life. Tonight, I felt that we were no longer alone. Even if Sean wasn't thinking about Linda, I was—her aura of sophistication was an almost palpable presence. And suddenly I found myself thinking about the other absent people who were also casting their shadows. I knew better than to ask about Linda, but felt I wanted to hear Sean speak, to break the spell.

"Do you know Molly's father?" I asked.

"I've met him."

"What's he like?" I pressed, although his tone already told me he wasn't in the mood to talk.

"Energetic. Well informed. Not the sort of person one gets to know easily."

"There's something I don't understand..."

"Really?"

This time his tone was just plain nasty, without the friendly teasing sound it used to have.

"It's just that Maria and Cheryl seem so different. It's hard to imagine the same person being in love with both of them."

"What makes you think he's in love with Cheryl?"

"Oh," I said.

"Poor Julia. You really are the last romantic. I don't know that he isn't in love with Cheryl—whatever that means—but I do know that being with a woman like Maria can be exhausting. All that intensity. Maybe Cheryl's a relief. And another thing. Cheryl may not set the world on fire, but she has one extremely important quality."

"What's that?" I asked.

"She's a survivor."

We both were silent after that. I wondered if he was thinking about Maria or about Linda. I was annoyed that he had called me "romantic." Actually I like to think of myself as cynical. Even I don't know what I meant by "in love." Heaven knows I don't have much evidence in my own life. Whatever my parents once thought about each other, all I've seen lately is familiarity that soured into irritation and hurt. And what the characters in *All Our Days* feel about each other seems like a bad copy of some dubious original.

When I left, Mrs. Holloway was in her vegetable garden, pouring beer into a pie dish. She must have noticed the look on my face because she said, "It's for the slugs."

"You feed them?" I asked, trying to keep the surprise out of my voice.

She laughed. "They're crazy about beer. They were destroying the garden. This way, they come for the beer, get drunk, and drown."

She held up another dish, filled with the bloated bodies of dead slugs. She seemed about to start a conversation, but I wasn't in the mood for more free advice and kept on going.

As I walked home, I kept seeing the bodies of those drowned slugs. I decided it was doing me good—a reminder of how things really are. Whatever I felt in Maria's garden, whatever I've sometimes felt with Sean, it's nothing you can grab on to. Not that anyone in their right mind would want to grab on to a slug—dead or alive.

As I was trudging down the road, lecturing myself about reality, I heard a car slow down and then stop. I looked up and saw Mabel watching me with what might have been amusement.

"I'd offer you a penny for your thoughts," she said, "but from the look on your face I'm not sure I care to know what they are."

"I was thinking about slugs," I said.

"That's kind of the way you looked."

"Mrs. Holloway was drowning them in beer."

"Yeah. That works. Except the way I look at it, the word goes out it's happy hour at the Holloways and you get even more slugs." She gave me a sharp look. "Mrs. Holloway, she's very good at what she does. And it's a good thing someone's keeping an eye on how we're poisoning this planet of ours. But some folks, that's all they think about. Some ways, it's easier to deal with bad things you can measure than with things you can't. Safer too."

"Safer?"

"Don't get disappointed that way...Sorry I missed you the other night," she added.

"How did you know I came by?"

"I have my sources." She smiled. "Was there something you wanted, sugar?"

"Not really. I just came by for a chat."

"Sorry I wasn't home, but you're welcome any time. Or any time there's something you want to talk over."

"Thanks," I said. "I'd like that."

"How's Molly keeping?" she asked.

"She's fine."

There was a long pause. I felt Mabel waiting for me to say something, but having convinced myself that there was nothing to worry about, I didn't want to reopen things.

"You take care now," she said, and I couldn't help feeling it was some kind of warning.

As I started down the road again, I became aware of the whirring of the cicadas. It sounded like the effects in a bad horror movie. I began by thinking it was funny, but after a while, the sound seemed to give substance to the darkness, and I was no longer certain of what was inside me and what was outside. What was Mabel warning me against, anyway?

Was it my imagination, or was the whirring becoming louder and more insistent? Suddenly it was blasted by the sound of backfiring. The next moment, Paul had stopped the scooter beside me.

"Want a lift?"

"Why not?" I said as casually as I could, to mask the fact that I was really glad to see him.

I climbed on behind him and put my arms around his waist. He kick started the scooter, and we zoomed off, bouncing over the bumpy road. The wind whipped my loose hair, stinging my cheeks, and the roar of the scooter drowned out the sound of the cicadas.

It was a relief not to talk and not to think, but simply to enjoy the thrill of hurtling through the night.

We reached Sandpiper Views long before I was ready to return.

"That was wonderful," I said.

"I'm glad you enjoyed it." He looked surprised at my enthusiasm. "We can do it again."

"Sure." But even as I said it, I knew I didn't want to do it again and I could see he recognized that.

"Catch you next time." And he vroomed off.

"Well, that's the end of that," I thought. "Who would want to be around someone who's friendly one minute and horrible the next?" And then I had to laugh. Paul and I probably have more in common than I'll ever let him know.

I actually like Paul, but how could I explain to him that even while I was enjoying myself on the scooter I had an indefinable feeling of loss? How could I explain that Sean's silences, even his black moods, make me feel more alive than Paul's most interesting conversation, when I don't understand it myself?

CHAPTER NINETEEN

August 26th

On the surface, everything appears to be the same. Molly and I sail and swim in the bay or pond. We chat to each other about this and that. And yet I have the feeling that neither of us is really there.

For the past two weeks, I have spent my time waiting for the days I have sittings, and my nights thinking about them afterward. But the fact of the matter is that nothing very much has happened. Sometimes Sean is nicer than other times. Sometimes I think, "Sean was wrong. Things can just continue." But beneath it all I am aware of a feeling of uneasiness, as if I am waiting for something to happen.

I did go for another motor scooter ride with Paul after all. Cheryl had taken Molly to the dentist in Hyannis, and I'd said I'd rather stay home. But once I was alone, I found I didn't know what to do with myself.

The day was still and hot. The house was filled with the sound of hammering and electric saws, and the beach was sure to be crowded. Suddenly, I knew exactly what I wanted to do.

I began walking toward the cemetery. I had never been there by myself, and I wanted to visit Maria's grave. As I entered the woods, I couldn't help thinking about going there with Sean, but I pushed away those thoughts. Today it was Maria who was on my mind.

The cemetery baked in the hot sun. There wasn't a breath of wind or the fluttering of a bird to break the stillness.

I stood for a long time in front of Maria's grave.

"What do you want?" I whispered. "Is it something about the house? Something about Molly? What do I have to do with it?"

Naturally there was no answer. Sunlight glinted on the flecks of mica in the granite. Green-headed flies settled on my bare arms and legs, stinging worse than mosquitoes. There wasn't even the glimmering of a response, the feeling of a presence that I had sensed in the house and garden.

As I started walking back, I swatted at the green-headed flies. Now I allowed my thoughts to turn back to Sean. What had changed after we walked to the cemetery, and why was he often so remote?

Just as I came to the main road, I heard the familiar sound of backfiring. I emerged from the woods just as Paul came around the bend. The scooter coughed to a stop.

"Hello again." He looked surprised to see me coming out of the woods. I wondered if he knew about the cemetery.

"It's so hot," I tried to explain. "I thought it might be cooler in the woods."

"The woods are cool—in both senses. There are old roads you couldn't drive on with a car, but you can on this."

We were both silent for a moment.

"Want to come now? We could explore a little."

"Okay." I didn't know I was going to say yes until I said it. "But I can't stay out long. Cheryl and Molly will be back soon."

I climbed on behind him again and we started back down the dirt road. I was glad when he took a turn to the left before we reached the cemetery. Somehow it didn't feel right to roar past it on the scooter.

We went deeper into the woods than I had ever been. Sometimes the road was so overgrown we had to get off and walk the scooter through. Sometimes the woods opened unexpectedly into a marshy area where startled birds scattered at our approach. The wind blew away the green-heads, and I told myself I was having a good time.

"This is great," I said as we climbed off the scooter to navigate some brambly things. "I didn't realize there was so much of the Cape that was unspoiled."

"Oh, it's there all right. If you know where to look. There are places in the dunes near Provincetown where it must be like what the Pilgrims first saw."

It was odd to hear him echoing things Molly had said. It was obvious that he too was drawn by this idea of another Cape. I could imagine spending what remains of the summer exploring with him. He's smart. He's interesting. He's easy to be with. And he doesn't touch my imagination.

As we made our way noisily through the woods, I thought about the unfairness and stupidity of it all. Just as my own inconsistency didn't seem to deter Paul, I knew that I would continue to be pulled by the shadowy space Sean creates, which, despite my better judgement, still seems charged with possibility.

I can no longer escape the fact that the end of summer is approaching. When we go into town, I can feel a kind of electricity in the air—a panic to catch whatever the summer had promised. For the tourists, the end of summer has spurred an attack of frenzied holiday making. There is an epidemic of beach picnics, cocktail parties, and tennis matches. People bake themselves in the sun and gorge themselves on lobster, like animals storing up for the winter.

On *All Our Days,* the characters are preparing for an end-of-summer barbecue and shopping for school clothes. Sandi is leaving Middletown to go to medical school. A new woman lawyer, Cindi, has shown up in town. Cheryl told us she is destined for a fling with Lance. I think she's boring and can't believe I'm sorry to see Sandi go, but Cheryl explained that her contract is up and she's been offered a part in an evening cop show.

Nothing more has been said about whether or not Molly is going to boarding school. Her father has been delayed again, but is due back the beginning of next week. I don't want to think about the winter myself, so it seems mean to ask Molly what is going to happen to her. On the one hand, it is probably better for her to get away from the house and Maria, but on the other, I can't imagine how she will survive wrenched away from them.

August 28th

I was surprised this morning when the phone rang and Cheryl handed it to me. Was it possible that by some delayed ESP, my mother was responding to the message I hadn't left on her machine two weeks ago? I couldn't think of anyone else who would call, unless it was Sean breaking a sitting appointment. At first I didn't recognize the voice that said, "Julia?"

"It's Paul, I have a favor to ask you."

"Me?"

"Yes, you. There's this dreaded dance at the yacht club. I'm expected to go, and I thought it might be just bearable if you'd come with me. It's tomorrow night. I know that's not a lot of warning, but it took me a while to get up my nerve to phone you. I know it's not your kind of thing any more than it is mine, but it would be a real act of kindness if you'd say yes. We could stand in a corner and sneer together."

"I'm not sure I can," I began. It was just about the last thing in the world I wanted to do, but there was something so recognizable about the way he had asked me, that I didn't want to say no either, so I added, "What time is it?"

"It begins at nine."

"I have something I have to do earlier, but I think I can probably get away. Can I call you back later?"

"Please say yes. We can make it up with a whale watch."

"I'll phone you later."

When I turned up for my sitting tonight, Sean seemed to have caught the collective jumpiness. He didn't paint with his usual concentration, and spent a lot of time just squinting at the canvas and taking a poke here and there. Finally he threw down his brush.

"I think this damn thing is almost finished. I

haven't captured what I wanted. But I'm afraid I'll screw it up if I overwork it."

"Can I see? Finally?"

"Not tonight. Let's do one more sitting tomorrow—just to see if anything leaps out at me. It's no good dragging things on. We'll say tomorrow's the last day. Sometimes a deadline helps."

Last day. I've known it was coming, but I still had a sinking feeling. And I didn't particularly like being thought of as something that was "dragging on." Well, it was a good thing it was coming to an end. I'd go to the dance with Paul after all and try to forget about it.

"I'll tell you what," said Sean. "You know most models get paid. Let me take you to dinner in Provincetown tomorrow night."

"I don't want to get paid," I mumbled.

"You silly goose. I didn't mean it like an obligation. I'd like to take you to dinner in Provincetown. Will you give me that pleasure?"

"Yes, thank you."

———

I told myself that Paul wouldn't really mind. But I could tell I was going to be wrong from the eagerness in his voice when I called.

"You can come? Great."

"No," I said, "I can't. My other plan is going to run longer than I thought."

"I see," he said, all the energy leaving his voice.

"I'm sorry," I said. "I really am." The fact is, I was actually beginning to feel sorry. I thought how rotten I would feel if I'd gotten up the nerve to call someone and they turned me down. Without a very good explanation.

"That's okay," he said. But I could tell it wasn't.

"Could we still go on a whale watch sometime?"

"Yeah, sure." But I have the feeling it's another opportunity missed. A real one, this time.

I felt bad for about five minutes after I hung up the phone. It isn't as if my life is full of invitations, and I really don't like hurting people. But tomorrow at this time I will be in Provincetown with

Sean. I think of the Fourth of July when I drove in to P-town with Cheryl and Molly and envied those sophisticated looking young women....

But I can't help having a kind of queasy feeling. The one law I know is that imagining something is a surefire way of making certain it doesn't happen. After all, I'm not some dumb character in a soap opera....

CHAPTER TWENTY

August 30th

As I came down to breakfast yesterday, I could hear Carly Simon singing about anticipation. While the words eerily echoed my mood, neither Molly or Cheryl ever began their morning to music. The mystery was soon solved.

The contractors had finally finished scraping the exterior. Two young men were listening to the radio as they began brushing on a creamy yellow paint. As much as I hated Cheryl's interior remodeling, I had felt that the shell of the old house was still intact—the scraping of the paint from the shingles only hastened the work of the wind and the rain. Now the yellow paint, not a bad color in itself, gave the house the pristine, preserved look of a restored inn or restaurant. However detached Molly seemed, she couldn't ignore this. But then I thought, "Tonight I will go into Provincetown with Sean," and that thought eclipsed anything else.

As I boiled water for tea, the Golden Oldie Hour was replaced by the local news. Announcements about a traffic accident in Dennis, a town meeting in Chatham, and a senior citizens chowder supper sifted through my dreamy consciousness without making much impression. As I took my first sip of tea, the announcer's voice continued.

"For the planetary minded, there will be an unusual occurrence. Tonight there will be the second full moon in the same month. For reasons that are not clear, this is called a 'blue moon.' Although undoubtedly related to the expression, 'once in a blue moon,' it is not certain which actually came first. Occasionally atmospheric conditions will give the moon a bluish cast, but that is unrelated to this phenomenon...."

"I didn't know there was really such a thing as a blue moon," I said to Molly. "I always thought it meant something so extraordinary it never happened. Like it had to do with the moon being made of blue cheese or something."

"Me too."

"Somehow it kind of takes the magic away."

"Yeah. I guess...."

I still blame myself. If I had not been thinking about my dinner with Sean, if I had not had a twinge of feeling bad about Paul, I might have watched her more closely. I might have been sensitive to her voice, and caught the fact that her tone of indifference had a studied quality. I should have been more suspicious when Molly looked at the yellow paint and simply shrugged. But her detachment suited me. I didn't feel like dealing with a temper tantrum today. In any event, I forgot about the blue moon almost immediately. It was an interesting anomaly of nature, like being able to balance an egg at the moment of equinox, but today my thoughts were elsewhere.

Molly was particularly sweet all day, trying to think of things I would like to do. Forgetting the lesson of the soap operas, and my own observations, I took it all as a good omen. A day beginning with Carly Simon singing my innermost thoughts, an unusual planetary occurrence, Molly's sweetness...For once it seemed as if everything was in tune.

The day passed with the incredible slowness of a day when you are only waiting for the evening, but at last it did come to an end. I had told Cheryl that I wouldn't be home for dinner, and I had the feeling that she connected it with Paul's phone call. I saw no reason to correct her, but I was a bit sorry that she was in the kitchen when I came down, dressed in the only dress I own. It's a black, flower-patterned, Betsey Johnson dress that has a low-cut elasticized top and a longish skirt. I can recognize the fact that it looks good on me, but I always feel like a bit of an impostor in it.

"Well, well," said Cheryl. "You're a sly thing. You didn't tell me you were going to the dance at the yacht club."

Of course I could have explained that the reason I hadn't told her was that that wasn't where I was going, but instead I just smiled and got out of there as fast as I could.

"Look at you," said Sean. He himself was just wearing a cotton sweater over some clean jeans, but he had shed the army jacket for the occasion.

"I just felt like wearing something different," I said, beginning to wish I'd never packed the filthy dress.

"You look very nice. Very nice indeed...And you've succeeded. You do look different...."

He didn't say it, but I had the strong impression that somehow he liked me better before. I would have given anything to be able to roll back time, the way you can rewind a videotape, to when I was getting dressed, and that I had put on something else.

"It's only a dress," I thought. "I'm still the same person." But I had a sinking feeling that something delicate had shifted.

I will never know if it was the dress itself, or my feelings about it. Or perhaps whatever there was between Sean and me was just too fragile to survive outside the world we had created in the studio. Whatever it was, it felt as if nothing I did was right, from the moment I put on the dress.

"Can I see the painting now?" I said.

"Afterward. Let's go."

As we turned down 6A, which followed the curve of the bay, I could see the lights of Provincetown sparkling in the distance. Above the silvery water, a fat moon hung in the sky, looking brilliant, but not very blue. I told myself that I was happy.

"Look at that moon," I said.

Sean looked.

The moon is so unfortunately linked with romance and dopey songs that I was afraid he might have mistaken what was actually a perfectly straightforward observation. So I began chattering very fast about how it was actually a blue moon even though it didn't look blue. But although he was usually interested in odd-ball natural phenomena, his attention seemed to be wandering, so

I trailed off in midsentence, and was silent for the rest of the trip.

We didn't eat at the restaurant I went to with Cheryl, but at an Italian restaurant. It was crowded with people who looked like the people in the first restaurant—sophisticated and vaguely artistic. Sean seemed to know a lot of them. They said hello and exchanged a few words, but although he introduced me, instead of feeling included in his world, it underlined my feeling that I didn't belong.

The food was probably delicious. I had veal with roasted red peppers and some homemade pasta, but I don't think I really tasted any of it. Sean was very nice to me, in the way that Molly was nice, making sure that I picked something special to eat and insisting that I try some of their zabaglione with fresh raspberries for dessert. But I had the feeling that we were working at making conversation, while before when we had talked we had rambled on and on, jumping from one subject to another as it occurred to us.

As we drove back to Truro, I once again wished that I could roll back time. The time I had spent imagining the dinner had actually been much nicer than the dinner itself. Although I knew I would replay the dinner again and again in my mind, there was not a great deal of substance to be gotten out of it. Anyway, the trouble with instant replays is that they don't alter the course of events.

When we got back to the studio, there was an old red MG parked in the driveway. I told myself there was no reason that Mrs. Holloway couldn't have a visitor, but somehow I didn't see her hanging out with people who drove classic sports cars.

"Damn," said Sean. "Linda."

I could feel the zabaglione beginning to curdle in my stomach. "I think I'll just go home," I said.

"Nonsense. I want you to see the painting."

He took me by the hand, but his grip felt tense instead of friendly and reassuring, and I felt as if I were being marched into the principal's office. Nevertheless, we entered the room hand in hand.

A woman was sitting at the table. She had made herself a cup of mint tea—what I had come to think of as "our tea"—and was reading an art magazine. She may not have been pretty, but she was certainly striking looking. Without the hat I could see that she had straight blond hair, art-fully streaked with a lighter color and set off by a tan.

"I didn't expect you," he said.

"So I see." She looked at me quizzically, and once again I wished I wasn't wearing that stupid dress.

"I'd like you to meet Julia, who's been sitting for me."

We both muttered hellos.

"You don't seem very pleased to see me," said Linda.

"You know I don't like surprises. Of course, I'm happy to see you. How was Paris?"

"A dead bore in August. It always is."

At that point I decided that I hated her quite objectively. I couldn't imagine being bored in Paris under any circumstances.

"Don't let me interrupt you," she said.

"There's nothing to interrupt. I was going to show Julia the painting."

"Oh, I'd love to see it."

I wanted to leave right then and there, but I didn't have the nerve. After waiting all this time, I certainly didn't want to see the painting for the first time with Linda. The old Sean, "not nice" as he may have described himself, would have known that. But this Sean seemed to have lost any sensitivity to my feelings. He took the canvas, which was leaning with its face against the wall, and put it on the easel.

A face looked out at me. It was definitely a face, not a bunch of shadows or abstract shapes, and I could see that the use of color was interesting. I suppose I recognized the features, but the girl in the picture looked much younger than I had felt in years, like a little kid, and somehow rather frightened.

"I like it," said Linda, after studying it for a while. "You've captured something—a kind of vulnerability and naïveté. It's rather touching. Quite a departure for you."

"It is, isn't it? I'm not quite satisfied with it, but I thought it was an interesting exercise."

I might just as well not have been in the room. I could feel tears beginning and was about to leave, when Sean turned to me for a reaction.

"Well?" he said.

"I'm sorry," I said. "I just remembered something. I have to leave," and ran out the door.

As I ran, I told myself that it was a good thing I was so mad, because it kept me from feeling utterly miserable. As the tears began to sting my cheeks, I reminded myself they were tears of rage. They weren't just directed at Sean and Linda, but at myself. For ever having been stupid enough to think someone like Sean could be interested in me.

When I reached the house, it was dark. I jumped as something rubbed against my leg. It was Tobermory. I leaned down to pet him, and then I thought, "Tobermory doesn't do that."

He stared at me intently, almost as if he were trying to communicate something. I continued to pet him, and then decided that I needed contact with more than a cat. I went upstairs to see if Molly was still awake.

The light was out in her room, but sometimes she lays awake staring at the ceiling. As I pushed open the door, I could see that Molly's bed was empty.

CHAPTER TWENTY-ONE

I ran down to the boat house, but I already knew what I would find. *Dawn Treader*, of course, was gone.

Above me, the sky was clear. The fat moon hung there, still not looking the least bit blue, but along the horizon I could see the fuzzy line of a fog bank. I told myself it looked thin and very distant.

I didn't, for one minute, think there was any supernatural danger, but a nine-year-old girl alone in a boat at night was danger enough. And it was all my fault. I had known the story. I had heard the radio broadcast. I had observed Molly acting more and more strangely. And I had been so preoccupied with my own imaginings that I had chosen to believe there wasn't a problem. I may not, like the governess in *The Turn of the Screw,* have actually conjured up the ghosts and literally frightened my charge to death, but I was just as much to blame.

I scanned the boats on the shore—another sailboat, a rubber life raft, a small motorboat tied to a mooring....

A thin wisp of cloud drifted across the moon, making it look like a Halloween card. Was it my imagination or had the fog bank moved in closer?

As much as I dislike motorboats, it seemed the most sensible choice. As I started to walk down to the water, something brushed against my leg. It was Tobermory again. He followed me to the edge of the bay, a darker shadow with gleaming eyes. As I began to walk out to the motorboat, he meowed. I turned and looked at him.

"What is it?" I asked. He meowed again. "You don't really want to come," I said. But when I reached down to pick him up, he didn't move away.

I waded back out to the mooring with Tobermory in my arms. When I reached the boat, he jumped down on the floorboards. I climbed in myself and stared at the outboard motor.

"Please," I murmured to whatever deity is in charge of mechanical things, "I don't understand about motors. I need this one to start. It's not for me. It's for Molly."

I had the feeling that I had only one chance. If it didn't catch the first time, it would flood or something and I'd never get it started. I put my hand on the cord.

"If you make this start," I bargained, "I promise that I'll read *How Things Work.*"

I yanked the cord. The motor coughed and hiccupped. I tugged again and the motor sputtered and caught.

"Thank you," I said to whatever powers were listening.

The motor was making a reasonably steady sound now. I adjusted the throttle and started out toward Billingsgate.

The moon still cast a bright light, rippling the water with silver, but I was aware of the darkness beneath me and around me. I didn't like the clouds that were now sliding more rapidly across the moon and the fact that the horizon was now completely obscured by the fog bank.

Tobermory crouched in the bottom of the boat, barely visible in the darkness except for his eyes. I fixed my own eyes on the lights along the shore and the distant lights of Provincetown as points of reference. I told myself that as long as I hugged the shore, I was reasonably safe. I had no idea when Molly had left, but I had no doubt about where she was heading.

I panicked as the shore lights suddenly disappeared. Then I pulled myself together.

"Idiot," I said to myself. "You're opposite Great Island. There are no houses." There was still enough moonlight to make out the silhouette of the dunes, and as I cleared the tip I could see the lights of Wellfleet Harbor behind me.

My feeling of reassurance vanished as I passed Jeremy Point. Ahead of me, where I ought to see the green flashing light beyond Billingsgate, was a gray blur. As if to emphasize the point, a fog horn hooted derisively at me. Somehow, treacherously, the fog bank had slid closer to shore.

The first thing I did was curse. The second

was to cut back the engine. I could still see immediately in front of me and several feet around me, but everything ahead was veiled in mist. Above, I could still see the moon and stars. They were of no use to me now, but I tried to remember their position for the trip back.

As the fog swirled and eddied around me, I felt a kind of loathing. It seemed to me as if all the unseen forces I had sensed playing around me had taken shape and the fog embodied everything that obscures light and direction. Somewhere in all the murk, Molly was alone in a small boat. All I wanted was to find her.

"What should I do?" I asked Tobermory, who was still curled, composed as ever, in the bow. The yellow eyes blinked. And then, suddenly, a light pierced the fog and vanished again.

"All right," I said, and edged the boat in the direction of the light. The mist had settled around me, chilling more than my body, and I waited for the light to flash again.

And then I realized what was wrong with the picture. I knew from the chart that the light off Billingsgate should be green, but this one was a pure white light. Tobermory's eyes glowed cold and opaque. Without giving it much thought, I had taken his companionship as a friendly gesture—as concern for Molly.

"It's not Molly, is it?" I said out loud. "You want to go to *her.*"

As if in answer, in the far distance, I could just make out the glimmer of a green light, which blinked on and off again. And then, nearer now, the white light flashed brilliantly through the fog. As I stared at the light that shouldn't be there, I could feel my senses begin to reel.

I struggled to hang on to my reason. If the illusory light indeed came from Billingsgate, I could turn away from it toward the shore. In fifteen minutes, I could be safe, but what about Molly?

I kept heading for the light. The fog was pressing closer now. I could only see a foot or two ahead of me.

"Molly!" I called out. But the trobbing of the motor masked any other sound. I reached out and cut the power. The boat continued to move toward the flashing light. I was spooked by this, until I remembered that when the tide was coming in, the current pulled toward Billingsgate.

As I continued to drift toward the light that shouldn't be there, I could feel myself giving in to the dream reality. There was an odd peacefulness to the surrender. Perhaps there had never been a choice. Perhaps from the very beginning those forces I had sensed had been pulling me toward this moment....

"Why me?" I asked Tobermory. But all he did was blink.

The water lapped gently at the bow as it pulled us forward. And then I heard another sound. A faint rhythmical splashing.

"Molly!"

The splashing stopped abruptly.

"Molly!" I called out again.

There was still no answer, but it seemed to me I could make out a darker shape in the murk. Tobermory stood up and put his paws on the gunwale. He was staring into the fog. I stared too until my eyes began to tear and I thought I saw a patch of something darker. There was only one oar in the boat, but I pulled it out and began to paddle.

The darkness finally resolved into the blurred silhouette of a small boat. As I approached, a sound boomed through the fog. It was the tolling of a bell.

Molly's face looked very white in the darkness. Her eyes were bright, but I couldn't tell whether it was with excitement or fear.

I reached out and grabbed her gunwale. The bell tolled again, solemn and ominous, and the light flashed brighter. I threw a line around a cleat on *Dawn Treader* and lashed the two boats together. Molly had turned away and was staring at the flashing light in a kind of trance. As I clambered into the tossing boat, there was a thump.

Tobermory had joined us. I climbed onto the seat beside her and put an arm around her.

"Molly, are you all right?"

She finally turned and looked at me.

"You see it too?"

"Yes," I said. "I see it."

"It's so beautiful."

I stared at the light. It was much closer now, and it seemed to me as if it was no longer the current, but the light itself that was drawing us toward it. The light pierced through the fog with a kind of awful beauty, and the bell continued its mournful tolling. I still couldn't make out anything in the fog, and I had no idea of where we were, but I felt as though I had somehow crossed to the other side of my fear. What, after all, was waiting for us back on shore? Sean and Linda… Cheryl and her home improvements…

As the light pulsed through the darkness, insistent and beckoning, I could feel it flooding me with its energy. I was beginning to merge with something for which there were no words, and as I did, I could feel my personality beginning to dissolve. Whatever it was that was Julia—the quirks and bad moods, fears and idiosyncrasies—was obliterated by the light that swept all the dark corners.

The swirling mist obscured the source of the light, but suddenly I knew that it did not come from any lighthouse. On the other side of the fog curtain, there wasn't a village with children playing and fighting, and dogs barking, but only the light itself, incandescent and annihilating….

A gust of wind brought the sweet scent of a meadow, but there was another smell as well. Tobermory made his chirping meow.

Molly turned to look at me. "She's waiting for us...."

And suddenly I heard a voice. It was inside my own head, but it was extremely distinct.

"Julia Johnson," it said. "You turn that boat around."

The voice was commanding, and somehow full of common sense. It was the kind of no-nonsense voice that speaks to a child, and it brought a comforting feeling like the smell of fresh baking.

Molly and Tobermory continued to stare at the light. It was blinding now, and I had to struggle to form my thoughts. In a moment there would be none left. Only the light itself. And suddenly I knew that I didn't want to find out what was on the other side of the mist. There was no denying the beauty and power of the light, but I was not quite ready to give up being me. Maybe there wasn't anything back on shore but hurt and humiliation, but "this series isn't cancelled yet," I said to myself. "I'm not ready to write myself out of the script."

Tobermory turned and glared at me.

"It's not over till the fat lady sings," I said to him defiantly. I climbed back into the motorboat and pulled the cord. The motor coughed and quit.

"What are you doing?" asked Molly, coming out of her trance.

"Shut up," I said. "Come on," I pleaded. This time, the motor caught.

"What are you doing?" Molly demanded again.

"We're going back," I said, and swung the boat around.

She called out something, but her words were blocked as I pushed the throttle ahead. I looked behind me, but she was hanging on to the side of *Dawn Treader*. At least she wasn't trying to untie my line.

I needed all my concentration now, trying to maintain my sense of direction, and looking above me for some glimpse of the stars. The fog still surrounded us, but it no longer seemed so cold. Like the little no-see-ums, it was annoying, but part of how things were, and I thought I would choose it over the light. Maybe I wasn't ready yet for all that clarity.

It seemed to me that the fog was beginning to thin, and then, as abruptly as we had entered it, we were out of the fog bank. Strung along the far horizon were the lights of Provincetown. It seemed a lifetime ago that I had had dinner there with Sean....I looked behind me. The fog still billowed, but it was unbroken by any light, and the bell was silent. Molly too was looking back. When she turned, I could see that her face was streaked with tears. She was holding Tobermory on her lap. She called out something that sounded like, "Traitor!" but I pushed the throttle forward and headed back as fast as I dared.

Soon among the lights along the shore I recognized the silhouette of the ugly houses. During my evening walks, I had commented inwardly on their use of electricity—every room lit like a Christmas tree and the most hideous outside lights. But tonight I was grateful for their excesses.

I tied the motor boat back on its mooring. As I began pulling *Dawn Treader* up on the beach, a shadow detached itself from the darkness.

"Good girl," said the voice I had heard in my head, and Mabel came toward us. She gave me a hug and then, in a moment, she had Molly in her arms. She put a blanket around her and handed me a shawl.

"It's weird," I said as we all dragged *Dawn Treader* into the boat house. "I thought I heard your voice out there, but I couldn't have...."

She gave me a look. "Don't talk now. Let's go back to my house."

Chapter Twenty-two

I am upstairs in my room now, where I began this notebook. Except that, instead of night, it is a bright, clear day with more than a hint of September to it. My suitcase is open on my bed, but I am not quite ready to start packing. Before I do, I feel I must get the last bits down, before they become blurred by the flurry of departure.

Mabel brought us back to her cottage, where she lit a fire and made us some cocoa.

"It was real," said Molly at last. "I saw it."

"Anyone here say you didn't?" asked Mabel.

Molly turned to me. "Why did you bring me back?"

I looked at Mabel. I didn't know myself. "I thought I heard you calling," I said again, "but it couldn't have really reached me."

Mabel just looked at me.

"Why did you have to bring me back?" Molly repeated. "It was so beautiful."

"Was it?" asked Mabel.

Molly didn't answer.

"It was frightening," I said at last.

"My mother was there," said Molly. "Calling me."

"You sure?" asked Mabel.

"She was very close."

"That's something else," said Mabel. "Could be it was something else she was trying to show you."

"Like what?"

"What did she tell you about Billingsgate?"

"That it was still there. In some other dimension. And if there was a blue moon, you could go back in time."

"And tonight?"

"It was true. If Julia hadn't pulled me back, I could have gone there."

Mabel looked at me. "Is that so?"

"I don't know," I said slowly. "I saw the light too, but somehow I had the feeling it didn't come from a lighthouse."

"What was it then?" demanded Molly.

"I don't know. It was beautiful, but frightening. It seemed to me that if we had followed it, we wouldn't have been able to come back."

"You make it sound terrible," said Molly, "like some kind of death. If it hadn't been for the light, you wouldn't have found me."

"That's true," I said. I turned to Mabel. "What do you think?"

"I wasn't there," she said. "Could have been lots of things." She turned to Molly. "Your mother loved you a lot, you know. Don't ever forget that. Could be she wanted to show you something... There are times when one thing's ending and another's beginning, and it's like the separation between things sort of slips. Almost like there's a crack in time—or between worlds...But it doesn't really take a blue moon to see that...."

"I don't understand," Molly began.

"What your mother was trying to tell you about Billingsgate is true. Just like that town is still there in its own way, so is your mother. She'll be with you as long as you remember her. But to be true to her doesn't mean you have to follow her. In fact, she needs you right here to keep her alive."

"There's nothing left of her in the house."

"The house is just a place she lived for a while. There's someplace else your mother loved, just as much as the house. Maybe more."

"The garden," I said, slowly.

"That's right," said Mabel. "Look after that garden."

Cheryl never even noticed that we had been gone. The house was dark when we returned. As we opened the door, something pushed past us. It was Tobermory. I had forgotten him down at the beach.

"You going to be all right?" I asked Molly, as I went upstairs with her.

"I'm okay."

"How about my sleeping in your room to-night?"

"Okay," she said again.

Lucy was skittering around her cage. She slept during the day and was most active at night.

"What about her?" I said. "How do you think she would have liked being left with Cheryl?"

"I didn't think of that. Poor Lucy." Molly took her out of the cage and put her on her shoulder. Lucy immediately began grazing on Molly's hair.

I crawled into the guest bed, crowded with stuffed animals. As I pulled up the blanket, Tobermory jumped on the bed. I decided there was no point in trying to figure out what went on in a cat's mind.

When Cheryl came downstairs the next morning, she looked unusually cheerful. I was afraid she'd come up with another idea for a fantasy sequence, but instead she said, "Guess what? Your father called. He's coming back this afternoon."

"He is?" Molly's face brightened.

I'd been so focused on Molly and Maria, that

I never thought about her missing her father. I knew I should be happy for her, and yet I had a momentary pang—as if something were over.

"Why don't you girls pick some flowers while I bake a cake?"

We went out to Maria's garden. The phlox had almost finished blooming. Orange butterfly weed and a bright red cardinal flower had appeared and a chrysanthemum bush was beginning to bud. The autumn colors changed the look of the garden. I missed the feathery pinks and lavenders of early summer. There were still some snapdragons that we could have picked for a bouquet, but Molly shook her head.

"There are some asters near the tennis court," I said. I didn't want to pick the flowers in Maria's garden either.

"I was beginning to think I was never going to meet your father," I said as we began to walk.

"Do you really have to leave so soon?"

"I have to get ready for school."

She made a face.

"Boarding school may not be so bad," I said. "Paul goes to one, and he's really okay. It could even be fun," I added, with as much conviction as I could.

"Will you write to me?"

"If you promise to write back."

"My spelling stinks."

"Mine isn't so hot either."

"You won't tell anyone, will you?" she said after a pause. "About Billingsgate, I mean."

"Of course not. It's something special between us. And your mother," I added.

"They can't take it away, can they?" she asked. "Not if we both remember."

"It's yours for keeps," I said. "Wherever you go."

When it was time to go to the airport, I said I'd rather stay home. I'm not big on family reunions, and I really wanted to be by myself and catch up on this journal. But as soon as I was alone, my thoughts and feelings began chasing each other around and it was difficult to find the right words.

At last I gave up and went out again to Maria's garden. It was different being there by myself. The fall flowers were more pungent, without the heady smell that had drawn me outside that night. Gradually I became aware of a feeling of sadness. At first I thought it was because the garden felt like the end of summer. And then I realized it was because the presence that had been strongest that night, but that I had felt from the first, was gone.

"Mabel lied," I thought. "She just told Molly that Maria was in the garden to make her feel better." And then I remembered that was exactly what I had thought when Molly had first told me the Billingsgate story. Mrs. Holloway would probably agree that it was a fairy story of the most dangerous sort. Cheryl too. But what about the light that I had seen with my own eyes? Deep down, whom did I trust, them or Mabel?

I stared at the sundial that said, "I count only happy hours." I still wondered how many hours it had counted, but then there was a lot that I didn't know. Probably I would never understand exactly what had happened, but I was quite certain of one thing—stirred by the changes in the house and because of Molly's need, Maria had been there for her. And for me too, I thought. Perhaps the garden wasn't empty of presence after all. It seemed to me that Maria was still there, but in a different way. Maybe having sent her message, and believing that Molly was going to be all right, she was somehow at peace. The fall flowers would die, but in the spring the lily of the valley and lady's-slipper would bloom again and the garden would be as I had first seen it. That, after all, is the great thing about gardens.

And then I found myself walking down to the beach. It was deserted except for a solitary figure.

"I didn't think you'd be here," I said.

"I was hoping you would be," said Sean.

I found myself with nothing to say.

"I suppose it's no use," he said, "telling you I'm sorry about last night."

"There's nothing to be sorry about," I said.

"Of course there is."

"I'm leaving in a few days," I said.

"I know that. And it's important to me that you don't go away thinking the wrong things…"

He lit a cigarette. Then stubbed it out.

"I'm not very good at this, but I'll try. I told you I wasn't very nice. And I'm not. I'm not even such a good painter. Mostly I'm selfish, and I used you. Not intentionally, and not in the way you imagine. You weren't a substitute for Linda. But you have a quality—of being untouched, I suppose—that brought something to me. I don't know what I brought to you, except some stiff muscles from sitting so long, and some hurt, which I truly regret—but I think that what we shared was a feeling of possibility...."

He stopped and lit another cigarette.

"I don't know if you know what I'm talking about, but I want you to believe it's not nothing. Perhaps, one day, you'll understand what I'm saying. The thing is that for now the gap between us is really too great. It could never have led anywhere other than where it did."

"It's all right," I said.

He looked at me closely. "There's something else, isn't there?"

"It has to do with Molly and Maria. I don't think I can talk about it."

"You don't have to. I can see that something's changed."

He looked at me thoughtfully. I had promised Molly I wouldn't talk about Billingsgate, but I had kind of meant to other kids at school. Somehow Sean was different, he was outside my ordinary life, and somehow he seemed part of the story too. He listened intently as I told him about the flashing light. When I told him how I had turned the boat around, he asked, "How come?"

"That's what Molly wanted to know. She was furious. I guess I just wasn't ready for wherever it would have taken us."

"Perhaps you never will be. And that's probably a good thing.... You're going to be fine, you know, although you don't think so. But I worry about Molly."

"Cheryl is pretty grim, and I don't know her father. But in any case, she's going off to school. At first I thought that would be terrible for her, but now I think it's okay. I don't think her connection with Maria depends on a place anymore.... And there's always Mabel. I think she's the most sensible person I know. Molly says she knows things, and it's true."

"I know that.... There's one other person you've forgotten. Someone you've underestimated all along."

"Who's that?" I asked, puzzled.

"Yourself, you goose. You know much more than you think you do." He stopped and looked at me for a moment. "It's funny, you know. Sometimes you remind me of Maria. But you're much more grounded. Keep that. But don't lose that other quality.... There's one thing I'd like you to try to get across to Molly. It always seemed to me that Maria's work was about trying to capture magic in the ordinary world. You know, it's possible to be true to her and still live in the real world."

"I kind of think Mabel was trying to say the same thing in a different way."

"That's all right then."

"Yes."

I traced a pattern in the sand with my toe.

"I guess I'd better be going." I said.

"Julia," he began. Then stopped. "Perhaps

there are things better left unsaid." He leaned over and kissed me on the forehead. "Take care of yourself."

"You too," I said. My forehead still burned from where he had kissed me, and I felt something beginning behind my eyes. I turned away quickly and began walking toward the stairs.

At the foot of the stairs, I turned and looked back. He was still watching me. I raised my hand in a kind of salute, and he waved back.

As I was walking up the road, I saw Paul coming toward me. I could see him recognize me, but as we approached each other, he looked away. I was afraid he might walk past me without saying anything.

"Paul," I said, as we came nearer, and put a hand on his arm to stop him. "I'm really sorry about last night."

"That's okay," he mumbled, and looked as if he was going to keep walking. Then he looked at me. "Say, are you all right?"

"Yes," I said, "I am." And I actually meant it.

"You don't really look it."

"It's more than I can explain right now," I

said. "I'm leaving in a few days....Is there any chance I could still go on a whale watch?"

"I think it could be arranged. How about tomorrow, if the weather holds?"

"I'd like that," I said. And I meant that too.

As I walked toward the house, the yellow paint glowed in the afternoon sun. The shutters had been painted black, and the effect was grand and a bit daunting. I had a pang of nostalgia for the house as I had first seen it. Dilapidated and forlorn, it had a feeling of romance about it, of a story waiting to be told. I thought that Cheryl could now use the house for an exterior if they ever had the budget to go on location. But if I am to believe Mabel, and Maria herself, then beneath the surface coat of paint, the spirit of the old house is still there, waiting for those who can see it.

I can hear a car approaching and turning into the driveway. It must be them returning from the airport. In a few minutes I will meet Molly's father. He's part of the story too. A piece of the puzzle. At least as far as Maria is concerned. But I feel as if my part of their story is over now. Despite what Sean says, I'm not even sure what my part in it was. Except I know that writing about it has helped. Especially the bits that were the most confusing and lasted the shortest time. Like Maria's photographs, perhaps the best you can do is try to catch things as they slip away.

I'm not sad. Really I'm not. I won't think about Sean. I won't think about leaving....I will think about the whales that I will see tomorrow— immense and mysterious, and almost accessible, ambassadors from below the depths....